A Plan
for Her Future

Lois Richer

LOVE INSPIRED
INSPIRATIONAL ROMANCE

LOVE INSPIRED®
INSPIRATIONAL ROMANCE

Recycling programs for this product may not exist in your area.

ISBN-13: 978-1-335-55433-8

A Plan for Her Future

Copyright © 2021 by Lois M. Richer

This edition published by arrangement with Harlequin Books S.A.

For questions and comments about the quality of this book, please contact us at CustomerService@Harlequin.com.

Love Inspired
22 Adelaide St. West, 40th Floor
Toronto, Ontario M5H 4E3, Canada
www.Harlequin.com

Printed in U.S.A.

"Love doesn't matter."

"Of course it matters!" Grace stared at him, confused, appalled and a host of other adjectives. "Marriage is all about love. What you're proposing sounds more like a—" She scrounged for the appropriate word and came up with "Partnership!"

"That's exactly what I want." Jack's head sank to his chest and his voice dropped.

"It sounds like a business deal."

"It will be. Sort of. We're friends, you and I. Nothing wrong with friendship," Jack insisted.

"Not a thing," Grace backtracked, wishing she hadn't let her stupid feelings take over. "Friendship is always a blessing. But if you are intent on pursuing this idea of marriage without love, it's better if we both start out with a mutual understanding about exactly what you expect from me."

Did she sound disappointed that he wasn't talking about love? Grace hoped not. She didn't want Jack to know how long she'd clung to that dream, or that, truthfully, even though she'd long ago given up on it, it still hung there, in the depths of her soul, yearning.

Lois Richer loves traveling, swimming and quilting, but mostly she loves writing stories that show God's boundless love for His precious children. As she says, "His love never changes or gives up. It's always waiting for me. My stories feature imperfect characters learning that love doesn't mean attaining perfection. Love is about keeping on keeping on." You can contact Lois via email, loisricher@gmail.com, or on Facebook (loisricherauthor).

Books by Lois Richer

Love Inspired

The Calhoun Cowboys

Hoping for a Father
Home to Heal
Christmas in a Snowstorm
A Plan for Her Future

Rocky Mountain Haven

Meant-to-Be Baby
Mistletoe Twins
Rocky Mountain Daddy
Rocky Mountain Memories

Wranglers Ranch

The Rancher's Family Wish
Her Christmas Family Wish
The Cowboy's Easter Family Wish
The Twins' Family Wish

Visit the Author Profile page at Harlequin.com for more titles.

To every thing there is a season,
and a time to every purpose under the heaven:
A time to weep, and a time to laugh;
a time to mourn, and a time to dance;
He hath made every thing beautiful in his time.
—*Ecclesiastes* 3:1, 3:4, 3:11.

This book is dedicated to those wonderful readers who have so faithfully read my stories. You send generous notes of encouragement and help. You lift my spirits with your kind comments and precious emails. You give love and compassion and bolster me on Facebook. You've blessed me so many times and I appreciate you very much. Thank you.

Chapter One

"Grace Partridge, you look stunning so stop fussing." Jessica James flipped up the car's visor, hiding the passenger mirror. "Trust me, with your makeup update, your stunning wardrobe and now that glorious feathered cut, you're going to be attracting men's looks the entire three months you're traveling the world."

"Oh." Grace gulped. *Attracting men's looks*— Did she really want that? "Maybe it's too much…"

"Out!" Jess laughed as she parked in front of Grace's tidy bungalow. She leaned across and flicked the door latch so the passenger door swung open. "No more second-guessing yourself. Embrace the new you, best friend of mine. And finish getting ready," she ordered after glancing at her watch. "The Calhoun boys will soon be here to drive you to catch your flight in Missoula."

"Yes, they will. Thanks for being my cheerleader." Grace hugged Jess, stepped out of her car and then she bent over to ask anxiously, "You will call me before I leave?"

"Try and stop me." Jessica sounded amused by her hesitancy.

"Thank you, dear friend. You are so—"

"I love you, too. Later, kiddo." With a cheery wave, Jess drove away.

Inside her home, Grace dropped her keys on the dish in the foyer while thinking how much she'd miss Jess these next few months. She hung the new dress she'd just purchased in the closet. What a lot of things she'd bought for this trip.

Actually, her wardrobe shift wasn't *only* for the trip. It was part of Grace's plan to shed the three D's: *Dumpy, Drab* and *Dreary.*

Her musing disintegrated at the sound of frantic pounding on her front door. When she pulled it open, her jaw dropped at the sight of a young girl whose face streamed with tears while she danced from one foot to the other.

"Help," she pleaded. "My pops is hurt."

Taken aback, Grace wondered when that nest of black hair had last seen a comb.

"Hey! Lady! Help him," the girl begged.

"Of course, dear." Grace snapped into action and grabbed her phone. "Uh, where is your pops?"

"There." The child pointed.

Grace gasped at the sight of a silver-templed man in a battered black leather jacket, lying sprawled on the street in front of an expensive-looking black car. She dialed 911 before racing outside and down her sidewalk toward the victim.

"I didn't see him, Grace," her elderly neighbor Mrs. Fothergill wailed as she stood by her car. "When I started backing up, he wasn't there. Then he was and my foot slipped on the gas pedal. Please help him."

"I'll try, Mrs. Fothergill. I'm reporting an accident." Grace focused on the operator and gave her address. "A man's been hit by a car. We need the ambulance and police. Hold on while I try to find out more about his condition."

Grace knelt by the man. He was unconscious. She pressed her fingers against his neck for a pulse. With his head half-buried under his arm she couldn't get a good look at his face. She was afraid to move him lest there were nonvisible injuries.

"Oh, Lord, help us," Mrs. Fothergill chanted repeatedly. Distracted by the feeble woman's agitation, Grace suggested she sit in her car and wait for help.

"Please, do something for Pops," the little girl implored her.

"I'm doing my best, dear." Grace studied her watch. "He has a pulse," she told the operator. "It's a bit fast. Yes, I do have first-aid knowledge, but I don't want to move him because his leg is at a strange angle. Also, there's a large bruise forming above his left eyebrow. I believe he hit his head when he fell so he may be concussed." She turned to the child. "Does your grandfather take medication?"

"He already took it," the girl explained. "I dunno if he's s'posed to take more."

Grace relayed that information and the name of the prescription on the vial she withdrew from the pocket of the leather jacket. The name suddenly registered.

"Jack?" she gasped in utter consternation.

The man moaned and moved his arm slightly, revealing his face. Grace gaped as her breath whooshed out.

He'd aged. His face was thinner, more angled, rendering him more rakish-looking than ever. But it *was* Jack.

The operator demanded to know what was going on.

"The victim's name is Jack Prinz," Grace explained after licking her dry lips and finding her voice. "He's fifty-three. Not from Sunshine. Not for many years."

She could hardly believe she was looking at her old school chum. Jack had been her first love when she was fifteen, until his father had suddenly moved the family to pastor a new church somewhere in Texas, leaving Grace heartbroken.

But other than their Christmas-card exchange, they had not kept in close touch. Which led her to wonder why Jack was here, now, in front of her house?

Just then his eyelids lifted. His beautiful golden eyes glinted with the same alluring charm they'd dazzled her with years ago when he'd coaxed her to forget her inhibitions and follow him in some wild new adventure. Perhaps there were a few shadows there she hadn't noticed all those years ago. Yet, despite the passing of decades, his eyes still reminded her of a wild tiger.

"'Lo, Gracie." His deep-throated growl hadn't changed either.

"Hello, Jack. Nice of you to *drop* by," she teased gently. He was the only person who had ever called her Gracie.

"Yeah." He grinned then winced. "Lizzie?"

"I'm here, Pops," the little girl assured him, striving hard to smile.

"What's happening now?" the 911 operator demanded.

"He's conscious," Grace said into the phone. "Just a moment, please." She touched his bruised forehead. "How do you feel, Jack?"

"Sore." He made a face, then joked, "Like a car hit me. Pretty sure my leg's broken. Shoulder's messed up, too. Everything seems to be spinning—" He groaned and closed his eyes.

The first responders arrived, so Grace rose and stepped out of the way as she passed on the information. That's when she noticed that the white-faced child had grasped her hand and was now clinging to it for dear life.

"Come with me, dear," Grace said gently.

"Let's sit on my steps. We can see what's going on, but we'll be out of their way. Okay?"

"O-okay," the girl agreed on the tail end of a sob.

Grace led the frightened child to her front entrance, sat beside her on the cool cement and then offered a fresh tissue. "Your name is Lizzie?"

"Uh-huh. Lizzie—uh, Elizabeth Prinz." Lizzie blew her nose, then sniffed. "Is Pops gonna be okay?"

"I think they're helping him." Grace hoped the child couldn't tell how worried she was. Jack looked pale and listless, nothing like the tanned, rebellious preacher's son she'd known in her youth. "How old are you, Lizzie?"

"Six." The child peeked through her lashes at Grace, sighed and then amended, "Almost."

"And why did your—er, pops bring you here? To Montana? To my house?" Grace waited, but when Lizzie didn't immediately speak, she speculated, "Maybe you were going to visit Glacier National Park?"

It seemed the most likely reason since Sunshine Township lay in the foothills, just outside the national park. With April's warm arrival, the alpine flowers would be blooming now. That was always a popular event in the park.

"Did you come to see the mountain flowers?" she asked.

"Uh-uh." Lizzie shook her head.

"Oh." Grace always liked to be prepared, doubly so now because despite the fact that she hadn't seen Jack in eons, her heart was thudding like a bongo drum.

Shock, she told herself. Hopefully the child had an answer to clarify this situation and maybe she'd give it before the Calhoun boys arrived to drive Grace to Missoula to catch that plane.

"If not for the flowers, why *did* you come?"

"So you an' Pops can get married," Lizzie announced. "So you can be my grandma."

Married! Grandmother?

Grace gulped. She'd never even been a mother! At fifty-two, maternity was a cherished wish, a years-long prayer she'd been forced to finally relinquish since God had never fulfilled her dearest desire to marry someone she truly loved or to create the family she craved. No way was she qualified to be a grandmother.

Which was the reason she'd focused on her second goal, the one she and Jess had planned together for the past five years. To travel the world.

Lizzie studied her curiously with Jack's tiger eyes. Her hair was like Jack's, too, that distinctive almost-black shade that shone in the sun like a raven's wing. Whether inherited or merely because she'd been with Jack a lot, the child also boasted the identical belligerent thrust to her jaw that her grandfather had employed way back when, a silent warning not to mess with him.

"You look funny," Lizzie said.

"Really? Because I feel funny." *Understatement*. Grace swallowed hard. "Lizzie, dear, I'm a bit confused. Um, why would your pops want to marry me?" She didn't add *now*, though she certainly thought it. Instead, she held her breath and waited for the answer as the unkempt child tilted her head to one side and stared into Grace's face, her golden eyes evaluating.

"Well, 'cause Pops wants you to help look after me." Lizzie's smile drooped as if she didn't want to say the next part. "He thinks I'm sick an' he thinks you'll know how to help me."

"*Are* you sick, Lizzie?" Grace asked quietly.

"I dunno." The child shrugged, grabbed a dandelion from the lawn and played with it. "Maybe. My heart hurts lots. But I don't think nobody can fix that."

Grace tried to fathom a reason for that comment. Why was Jack here with his granddaughter? Where were Lizzie's parents? There seemed only one answer—gone.

To Grace it felt as if the spring sunshine suddenly dimmed and the chirping birds fell silent. An orphaned child. How sad. She'd lost her own parents when she was an adult and it still hurt. Poor Lizzie wasn't even six years old!

"We're taking Mr. Prinz to the hospital, Miss Partridge," Carmen Brown said. She had been an EMT for ten years. Actually, Grace had helped pay for her training, though Carmen didn't know that and Grace had no intention of telling her. It was enough that Carmen was very good at her job.

Grace rose so that she and Carmen were on a level plane. Hopefully Lizzie wouldn't overhear them.

"Will Jack be all right?" she murmured.

"Think so," Carmen said with a nod. "Eventually. He's in some pain. My guess is he broke his leg. Maybe his foot, too. His shoulder's paining him. Might also have a cracked rib. And he's lightheaded. We'll transport him to the hospital so they can run some tests. They'll probably keep him overnight for observation."

"Oh, dear." Grace swallowed. She was supposed to be leaving town!

"The police are with Mrs. Fothergill, so you can follow us in if you like, Miss Partridge," Carmen said. "But you'll probably have to wait to speak to the patient and the doctor."

"I wanna go with Pops," Lizzie insisted, trying to push between them.

"You can't, honey." Carmen grasped the child's arm. "He's going to the hospital in the ambulance, with me. We can only take sick people in the ambulance."

"Your grandfather needs a doctor to tend to him now. We'll follow in my car, Lizzie." Grace decided immediately. "But first we'll see if we can help Mrs. Fothergill, and I'll okay you coming with me without a car seat. Since it is an emergency." She smiled at the child. "Then we'll find out what's happening with Jack. When we know that, you and I will decide what to do next. Will that be all right, dear?"

"'K." The answer took a while to emerge from the forlorn-looking Lizzie. She flopped onto the step, propped her elbows on her knees and huffed a sigh of resignation. But her gaze remained on the ambulance and her grandfather lying inside it.

"Thank you for your help, Carmen." Grace waited until the EMT hurried away. A moment later, the ambulance left. "Wait here please, Lizzie. I'll be right back."

"'K."

Grace checked on Mrs. Fothergill. Reassured the police had everything under control and once she had permission to transport the child in her vehicle without a car seat, she returned to Lizzie. The little girl wore too-small jeans with ragged holes in the knees that were from use and not some designer fashion statement. She had sneakers with ratty laces, no socks and a T-shirt that bore a wealth of evidence about her recent meals.

What now?

Grace felt, as her father used to say, *at sixes and sevens*. This was *Jack's granddaughter* and that sent her into thoughts of the past. Until she realized Lizzie was again holding on to her hand in that death-grip.

Oh, Lord, what am I to do with this child while Jack's in the hospital?

"Hey! That looks like Pops's truck," Lizzie said. "Only he sold his."

That's when Grace noticed a red half-ton truck moving toward her with the logo of Hanging Hearts Ranch emblazoned on the side. The Calhoun boys!

"I forgot all about them," she muttered, dismayed that Jack's reappearance and her silly fluttering heart had knocked her so off-kilter that for a moment she'd forgotten her upcoming trip.

"Who are they?" Lizzie gaped at the three tall, very handsome brothers now hurrying toward them.

"Very dear friends." Seeing the brothers' expressions of concern produced a flush of warmth inside Grace. They were so precious.

"You okay, Miss P.?" The eldest Calhoun brother, Drew, scanned her face.

"Who's this?" His brother Zac smiled at Lizzie.

"What happened?" Sam, the youngest, glanced around as if looking for answers.

As quickly as she could, Grace introduced them to Lizzie and then explained the situation.

"I'm guessing you don't want to leave for your trip until you have more information about your friend." Drew nodded understandingly.

"Well, yes." Grace couldn't shake off her sense of bemusement. *Marry her?* Lizzie couldn't be right.

"Uh, Miss P.?" Drew nudged.

"Sorry, dear. I was thinking." She pulled herself together to focus. The Calhouns had called her Miss P. for ages. Once she hadn't liked it, but now it seemed like an endearment. "I'm a bit uncertain about what to do next."

"Why don't you lay it out for us?" Drew advised. "Maybe we can help."

"Well, since I am to be away for three months, I've rented my house. The little family is moving into my home tomorrow morning. I've just had the entire place professionally cleaned in preparation and the carpet is still a bit damp. Anyway, I can't stay here tonight because I won't have time to launder linens and such because I'd have to leave so early in the morning." Grace stopped to catch her breath.

"Hmm. There are some issues," Zac agreed.

"Yes, because my bags are all packed and the hotel in Missoula is reserved for tonight," she clarified. "I'm supposed to leave now, with you, but—oh, everything is a mess."

"Never mind any of that right now," Sam soothed, patting her shoulder. "Hotels will wait. You and Lizzie need to go to the hospital and see about your friend before you decide anything else."

"Yes," she agreed, but her stomach pinched at the prospect of seeing Jack again. Would he think she looked okay or…?

"Let's do this." Zac had always been the trio's

best problem solver. "We'll take your bags, and Lizzie's, to the log house at Hanging Hearts Ranch." He checked with his brothers, who nodded their agreement. "You and she can stay there as long as you need or until you decide your next move."

"That's kind, thank you, dear. But what about my trip? We were driving in tonight so I could fly out tomorrow morning," she reminded them.

"You decide about that after you get more information. We'll take you no matter when you want to go." Drew leaned forward and gave her a hug, which would have been unusual when he was younger, but he'd softened since he'd come back to live with his family at the Double H, as locals called the ranch. "Lizzie can come home with us now, if you'd prefer that."

"No! I gotta see Pops," Lizzie wailed. "Afore he dies. She said—" the child pointed at Grace "—we could go."

"No one is dying, dear," Grace soothed the little girl. "The doctors will help Jack get better. I did say that we'd go to the hospital and I still think it's the best course of action for both us and Jack. He'll want to know Lizzie is taken care of. The police have given permission for her to ride with me even though I don't have a car seat for her."

"There's one in the truck you could use." It took

Drew only a few moments to transfer the seat from their truck to her car. "Okay now, Miss P.?"

"Yes." Grace smiled at the Calhoun brothers. "Thank you for your help, boys. Lizzie and I gratefully accept your offer of the log cabin, for tonight at least. I think."

The Calhouns looked at each other with expressions that Grace understood only too well. They thought she was old-fashioned for calling them boys when they so clearly weren't. But they'd always been boys to her. Her adopted sons. Perhaps not in the truest sense, yet she *had* adopted them into her heart, prayers, thoughts and actions years ago, after they'd arrived in Sunshine as bereft children who had just lost their birth parents in a horrible car accident.

When her friends Ben and Bonnie Halston had legally adopted the three brothers and taken them to live on their Hanging Hearts Ranch, the Calhoun boys, like so many other folks in and around Sunshine, had become part of Grace's life. She'd taught them Sunday school, how to use the library, prayed for them, and watched them grow and change.

In fact, over the years, the entire town of Sunshine had become her family, the one she'd never had. She'd lived a full life here. But tonight she was leaving this town and the people she knew and cared for, to see the world.

Except—what about Jack? And Lizzie?

"Okay, here's the plan." Sam raked a hand through his hair. "You and Lizzie get going. If you need anything, you call us. We'll be waiting to hear about your friend and to take you to Missoula whenever you're ready."

"By the way, Miss P.," Drew murmured with a wide smile. "You're looking really stylin' with that new hairdo. *Trés* chic!"

"Why, thank you, Drew. Thank all of you for helping me." She tried to quash her blush, but they saw it and grinned. They were such special men. Each one hugged her, patted Lizzie's head before loading the luggage, Lizzie's as well as the overnight case Grace had left inside her house, already packed for her trip. They drove away with a wave.

"They're nice," Lizzie said. And then, "Can we go see Pops now?"

Was that what she wanted? To see Jack again? There was no other choice.

Grace led the way to her car, helped Lizzie into the backseat and waited until she'd done up her car seat belt. Thank the Lord this child would be safely secured for however long she was staying.

Staying? But—

"Here we go to the hospital," she said gaily as she drove out of her garage, ignoring the voice in her head that kept asking why she had to get involved. "We're off to see your pops."

But still Lizzie's words circled in her brain.

So you an' Pops can get married. So you can be my grandma.

Grace needed some privacy to talk to God before she talked to Jack about *that*.

Jack blinked in confusion. Then, slowly, he remembered.

He was in the hospital. Late afternoon sunshine poured in through a big picture window overlooking a verdant green valley that was at least as lovely as the view on his Texas ranch had been.

A noise nagged at him. Jack tilted his head toward the source. The pain of that motion made him wince, but he saw that he was hooked to a monitor that beeped his heart rate. His fingertips touched the nasal cannula that fed him oxygen. When he tried to shift, one leg felt very heavy.

"Hello, Jack."

He knew that voice, knew the soft, quiet tone of it, gentle, unhurried, kind. He eased his head to the left and let his eyes feast on the woman occupying an armless chair. She looked as elegant and balletic as she had almost forty years ago.

"Hello, Gracie." His throat was dry, making it difficult to speak. She obviously understood his plight for she immediately rose, took a glass off the nightstand and held the straw to his lips.

"Slowly," she murmured. "Just a little. You had surgery on your foot and they don't want you to drink a lot yet." When he'd taken a sip, she replaced the glass and returned to her seat. "How are you feeling, Jack?"

"I'm fine. Where's Lizzie?"

Jack really hoped she hadn't called a social worker or someone for his granddaughter. Though he'd messed up the grandparenting thing repeatedly, so far he'd managed to avoid unwanted attention from do-gooders.

"Lizzie is with one of the staff at the moment. She's having a snack. You're not allowed more than one visitor at a time." Gracie's smile had always made him feel better. "Your granddaughter is a remarkable child, Jack."

"That she is." He knew from the glint in Grace's perceptive purple-blue eyes that Lizzie had spilled the details of why they'd come to Sunshine. Given her pursed lips, he was pretty sure his former high-school girlfriend didn't approve. "How have you been, Gracie?"

"Very well." She didn't alter her gaze. "And you?"

"Learning how to manage, I guess," he said, the pain of loss still fresh. "Since my son Cade and his wife died six months ago, Lizzie and I have been trying to figure out life." He paused, then admitted, "That's why I came to see you."

"I'm so sorry for your loss, Jack," she responded gently. "And for Lizzie's." The way she said it told him she guessed that he'd deliberately left that information out of his last Christmas card. "You've been raising Lizzie on your own?"

"Yes. I'm lousy at it, but she's a sweet kid and doesn't complain." Jack eased his head into a more comfortable position and sighed. "She gets the short end of the stick having me for her grandfather."

"You thought I could help?" Grace met his gaze squarely. "I can't image why."

"Despite the fact that we haven't seen each other in years, I *know* you're the only one who *can* help us. I've read and reread those newsy Christmas letters you faithfully send every year." He caught her skeptical expression and quickly added, "Even though I didn't say much in return."

"Nothing. Except for a signature. And so?" She tilted her head in the same imperious way she had done all those years ago, silently compelling him to explain.

"And—" Jack felt weak and vulnerable, and he hated it. Which was even more reason to get this said before he wimped out. Funny how his great idea didn't seem so great right now.

"I'm listening," she chided quietly. "Go on, Jack."

"Your letters affirmed what I already knew. You have the kind of heart Lizzie needs, Gracie." The words poured out of their own accord. "I'm still no good at listening to inner voices, but I figured God was sending me here."

"Well, I wish He'd given *me* a heads-up," she said with some asperity.

That was such a Gracie-answer. Jack couldn't help it; he burst out laughing, then wished he hadn't when fierce pain shot through his shoulder and side. He inhaled slowly and then exhaled as the pain began to ease.

"Jack?" She sounded worried.

"I'm fine. Damaged something, maybe a rib? I forget the diagnoses. Anyway, it only hurts when I laugh."

Jack had no idea what to call her hair color. No longer the soft brown of their youth. For sure not gray. Not blond, either. Platinum, maybe? Whatever. That combined with the short, wispy style, suited her wide smile. Add those expressive purple-blue eyes and Gracie was a knockout.

"Jack?" She arched her brows when he kept staring. "Do you need a doctor?"

"No! I've seen enough of them." He almost shook his head, but then remembered it would hurt. "I used to ride broncs. I'm tough." *Pathetic, Prinz.* "Can't help it if I'm gawking, Gracie. You're stunning. Like a model or something."

"Oh. Well, thank you." She bent her head as she said it and smoothed one hand down her black-and-white houndstooth jacket, which had probably been specially tailored for her. He recalled she'd used the same gesture years ago when she was embarrassed by a compliment. "What really brought you to Sunshine, Jack?"

"I'm sure Lizzie already told you. She's not great at keeping quiet." Gracie's eyes held him captive. "I'm probably ruining your fancy world by coming here, but I didn't know who else to turn to."

"Turn to for—?" She calmly folded her hands in her lap and waited.

Her perfectly shaped nails were tinted the palest shade of pink. So elegant. Like the rest of her. More doubts crept in. This stylish woman wasn't the girl he remembered, the one who hadn't cared much about style. Maybe…

"I was going to ask you to marry me," Jack blurted before he thought better of his plan. Grace said nothing though her eyes intensified to an even darker purple. He hurried on. "Lizzie's not doing so well since her parents died. She hardly talks. She doesn't want to be around other kids or play or anything. My parenting skills haven't made things better. In fact, I'm probably making them worse somehow. I'm a lousy grandfather."

"Lizzie loves you," Grace said. He was glad she'd noticed.

"Yeah, but that makes it harder." Questions filled her eyes. No dodging now. It was time to explain. "I'm as bad at being Lizzie's grandfather as I was at being Cade's father. And I'm not thirty-five anymore so if something happens to me…" He let it trail away.

"Lizzie's afraid of that?" Gracie frowned. "Or you're sick?"

"I'm in perfect health. Or I was when I got here," he added huffily. "But of course Lizzie's afraid. She's got nobody but me. No one she can be sure will be there for her. Today—" Jack imagined the accident scene and grimaced. "Me, lying on the street, passed out, must have really scared her. Probably reminded her."

"Of?"

"Losing her parents. One day her mom and dad were there. The next they were gone, killed in a diving accident off the coast of Bali." Grief tugged at him but he refused to give it room. "Losing family—it's like a bad dream you want to wake up from. Only Lizzie can't wake up from this loss and she's struggling to deal with it."

"Because she fears that if you're gone, she'll be all alone." His old friend nodded. "I get it."

Inside, a bit of tension dissipated. He'd known Gracie would understand.

"Such a loss has to be very difficult for both of you," she added softly.

"I could handle it if Lizzie was okay. But she isn't." Jack shook his head. "And I'm not helping her. Or maybe I'm not doing it right. What do I know about little girls?"

"Surely girls aren't that different at this age

from little boys, like Cade was. Are they?" she asked.

Admitting the truth was going to reveal the ugliness of his marriage, but Jack had decided before they'd come that he was willing to be so exposed if it would make Gracie understand.

"I don't know." Her eyebrows arched in enquiry. "I messed up there, too," he admitted. "Cade and I didn't really connect much when he was a kid."

"Sort of like you and your dad," she murmured.

"Yeah." He hated saying that. "Cade had more in common with his mother." At least, that's what Sheena had claimed. But Jack wasn't going there, not just yet. "Lizzie hasn't got anyone but me now. When I blow it, she never tells me I'm wrong or dumb or off base. All she says is, *It's okay, Pops.* Then she goes into her room, closes the door and lies on the bed, hugging the stuffed animal her parents gave her last year."

"Maybe if you got her engaged in something—"

"I've tried!" Jack exclaimed. "I've tried everything I can think of. Before her parents died, she'd been learning to ride. She loved it." Jack sighed heavily. "Now I can't even get her to pet a horse, let alone ride one."

"I see." Gracie studied him seriously. "But how would marrying me help Lizzie? The child doesn't even know me."

"Yet," he added with a grin. "But when she does, she'll love you. Everyone does. I remember how you were always like a magnet to the other kids."

"Jack." Gracie was so serious. "This isn't school. Things have changed."

"They have," he agreed with a nod. "But not basic character, and certainly not yours, Gracie Partridge. I predict that within the week, Lizzie will be eating out of your hand."

"I hope not." She wrinkled her nose in distaste before getting back to business. "If you intend on living in Sunshine, Lizzie and I will see each other. I'll naturally do whatever I can to help her get over her loss."

"That's kind and I appreciate it," Jack said sincerely. "But it isn't enough. My granddaughter needs a mother, somebody to love her." *Better than I can.*

"Her mother is gone, Jack. I could never take her place. I don't want to." Gracie didn't have to use words, her expression chided him for saying it.

"That came out wrong. I meant to say she needs a *grandmother*." He watched her lovely eyes narrow.

"What about your wife?" Gracie met his stare head-on. "Sheena, wasn't it? Surely she fits this role better than I do."

"I thought I'd told you..." Jack licked his lips

when she shook her head in a firm *no*, knowing he'd deliberately *not* told her because he wanted to forget all the ugliness, all the pain his marriage had entailed.

"You never said much of anything in your scribbled cards," Grace said.

"Sheena passed away several years ago. Breast cancer." Jack had deliberately withheld putting details about his life in those cards.

Why he'd done it was a confusing mix of answers. It was probably tied up with his memory of their relationship all those years ago and how happy he'd been with Grace. Or perhaps it was due to the vividly happy word pictures she'd painted of her life, while his had slid downhill to rock bottom after he'd left Sunshine. Perhaps he'd worried that if she knew the truth about his failures, Gracie would have been disappointed in him. But more likely it was that hidden, but longstanding fear that she'd remember he'd once told her he loved her. And he had.

But love wasn't something Jack had allowed himself for a very long time. Love made you weak. Thanks to his father, he'd learned he was unlovable. Sheena had taught him that it cost too much to want to be loved, to bare your soul and have it crushed by lies, cruelty and anger. Love exposed you to unfathomable pain. It was better to hang on to your pride and dignity, to be strong, independent and unfettered by that emotion.

"Jack? You've gone awfully quiet. I'm sorry if I revived sad memories—"

"You didn't. I'm really tired, Gracie," he interrupted, unwilling to cry on her shoulder about his past and see pity for him darken her lovely violet eyes. "Maybe you should go now. We can talk about this tomorrow."

"But Lizzie wants to see you," she reminded him, appearing confused.

"Let her peek in for a minute, but just a minute." Jack leaned against the pillow, in pain and suddenly more worried than he'd been since he'd come up with this wild idea.

What if Gracie wouldn't marry him? What would he do then?

Chapter Two

"Have you gone crazy, Grace Partridge?" Jess stared at her, obviously stunned.

"I don't think so, dear." Having missed her usual evening snack, Grace calmly poured herself another cup of tea.

"You're going to marry Jack, whom you knew many eons ago—because he needs someone to look after his granddaughter?" Her friend shook her head in disbelief before adding, "You're going to give up the trip of a lifetime for a man you haven't seen since you were, what, fourteen?"

"Fifteen. And it's far too premature to discuss marriage. I'll need to give that much more thought." Grace calmly took another bite out of Jess's freshly baked coconut cookie and complimented her on it before explaining. "Anyway, I'm not *giving up* the trip of a lifetime. I'm giving that trip *to you*."

"You can't. It's way too expensive. I'll never be able to pay you back."

"I don't want you to pay me back. It's a gift," she said and smiled.

Jess simply stared as she'd always done when

Grace relayed one of her *perfect* plans. "You can't do it!" she insisted.

"I already have. The money doesn't matter. You know that distant relative in Poland left me well off. The truth is, I'm going to enjoy hearing you describe everything you see." Grace smiled at her. "I've spoken to my travel agent, Jess. It's all been changed to your name. She's even dealt with the travel insurance."

"I'm sure there's a costly change fee. There always is," Jess argued, looking flustered. "And even if they waived it, I don't have anything packed. I can't just drive to Missoula tonight, stay in a hotel and take a plane out of the country tomorrow morning. It's—impossible!"

"It's actually quite doable. You and I are the same size. We like the same colors. So, you'll wear my new clothes. Everything is already packed. If you need something else, you can buy it along the way. But you won't need a thing except souvenirs," Grace predicted.

"But I, I mean you—" Jess stopped.

"Thankfully," Grace said, interrupting whatever objection Jess was about to make. "You and I planned thoroughly when we intended to take this trip together. You know every detail of it. All you need to pack are your personal care items. And your passport. Isn't it a blessing that both of us got our passports before we learned you'd have to cancel and give your trip money to help your son with medical bills? Now you can just go."

"Grace, this is—"

"The perfect answer. I'll look after your house, water your garden, make sure everything's fine. You'll text me about where you are and what you're doing and send me pictures." Grace smiled as if it didn't bother her one whit to give up this dream. Jess would see past her bravado if she didn't put on a good show. "Lots of pictures."

"But—" Jess stared at her. It was the first time Grace had known her friend to fall speechless.

"We *will* share our trip, dear," she promised. "Only in reverse of what we'd planned. Now let's not waste time arguing. The Calhoun boys will soon arrive, ready and willing to drive you to Missoula. You should get there in time to catch some sleep before the flight if we don't lollygag." She rose and beckoned. "Come."

"Grace, I can't let you do this, not for Jack Prinz," Jess argued. "You've talked about this trip forever."

"Yes, *we* have. And I am going to enjoy every moment of it, provided you do your part." She added rather severely, "Besides, I'm *not* doing this for Jack." *Not totally true*, her brain squealed, but she ignored it. "Get up, girl. Let's move."

Though Jess continued to dispute the decision, Grace refused to listen. She'd made herself a final checklist days ago and she went through it now, ensuring every detail was covered so her friend would have nothing to worry about. She even managed to slip the extra cash she'd withdrawn this morning into Jess's wallet without her friend noticing. She'd already arranged for her travel agent to add to Jess's onboard credit for some spa pampering on the cruise part of the journey. Now there were only mere details to work out and those were easily arranged.

"It was a real blessing that Drew's wife, Mandy, offered to stay with Lizzie at the log house on the ranch so I could help you get ready. Oh, here's a text." She glanced at her phone. "The Calhouns are outside, waiting for you. They have your new luggage loaded."

"Already?" Jess gulped. "Everything's happening so fast."

"But it's all good." Grace held out her arms. "Enjoy your trip, Jess, dear. Send me lots of texts and pictures and postcards."

"I feel like I'm in a cyclone," her friend murmured as they hugged. "Are you absolutely sure about this, Grace?"

"I have a deep inner assurance that staying is the right thing for me to do." Well, she *hoped* she'd have that, and soon. "Since I can't leave Lizzie with Jack while he's recuperating, it seems silly to let the trip we planned go to waste. Doesn't it?"

"I guess." Her friend finally nodded, seeming bemused.

"It does. Now it's time to leave." Grace walked Jess to the truck where the Calhoun brothers promised they'd take good care of her and make sure she got on her plane the next morning. After one more last-minute check, she handed over her new phone. "The Calhouns helped me find a SIM card that lets you use this anywhere, so don't be stingy with your photos." She smiled as Jess teared up. "Oh, hush now."

"How do I ever thank you, Grace?" her best friend burbled. "I never in a million years thought I'd get this chance—"

"You thank me by enjoying yourself." They hugged once more. "God speed, Jessica."

"Keep me up to date with you and Jack," her friend whispered in her ear. "And don't get married till I get back." Jess winked. "Bye."

Married? As if that would happen.

Grace watched the Calhoun brothers escort Jess into the truck. Then she waved until the vehicle disappeared down the street. When at last she was alone, the chill of the spring evening air penetrated and it suddenly struck her. This was the first time in as long as she could remember, that her dear friend wouldn't be right there if she needed her. Grace already felt lonely.

Shivering, she returned to Jess's house, turned off the lights and locked up. Then she drove back to Hanging Hearts Ranch and the log cabin where she and Lizzie would stay for—how long? She had no firm date and Grace hated uncertainty. She preferred neat, orderly plans. During the drive she tried to mentally organize her next moves, but the sheer scope of issues to be dealt with threatened to overwhelm her. Talking to God had always been her way of sorting through complications. So, even though lately He'd seemed distant and silent, she tried again.

"I don't know if sending Jess was the right thing, Lord. But I didn't know what else to do."

Grace faced the whole truth then, which was that Lizzie wasn't *really* her problem. Yes, it was nice to help the poor girl, but perhaps inside her heart she'd actually chosen to stay because something had glimmered in Jack's sad eyes when he'd spoken about his wife. Something that seemed like regret and pain had deeply moved her. She had a hunch his marriage had disappointed him, though why she thought she could help that was a mystery.

Maybe this curious pull she felt, this strange urge to get to know Jack again, this need to re-friend the boy she'd never quite forgotten, lay behind her decision to give Jessica her trip, the very one that was supposed to help her rediscover God and His plan for her future. Retiring from the library hadn't fulfilled her the way she'd expected. Grace was young, energetic. She needed to be involved in something.

But why did she feel she must help Lizzie? Jack

wasn't going to turn into some long-lost love after all these years. He was different now. There was an edge, a hardness to him that time and circumstance had wrought. Was she hoping to alter that? The thought so unnerved Grace, she shut it down and returned to praying.

"The deed is done now, so I need You to show me the next step because I don't know what to do. I haven't known Your will for me for a while." She pulled up in front of the log house, gripped the steering wheel and exhaled. "Am I following Your plan now?"

No response.

Hanging Hearts Ranch appeared ethereal in spring's late twilight with the sun fully set and the first twinkle of stars flickering above. The soft whinny of horses in the paddock floated through the air, the fresh clean air filling her nostrils.

"Is this what You want me to do?" Grace didn't feel a familiar flutter of peace inside her heart as she got out of her car and surveyed the sky. "I'll care for the child, but I need reassurance that this is Your will for me."

From behind a stand of evergreens, the sliver of a moon peeked out at her. But no confidence or clarity emerged with it.

It seemed God was telling her to wait. Just as He had when for years she'd prayed He'd send someone to love her.

* * *

Jack scowled at Dr. Fritz's retreating back.

So now he'd be stuck here a third night, and all because he'd had a little wobble at lunchtime. Well, okay, he'd blanked out. But only for a few seconds. Maybe a minute! But he had to get out of here. He had to get things settled with Grace.

"Good afternoon, Jack." As if conjured up by his thoughts, Grace stood in the doorway. Like that, his weariness vanished. Stunning in gray slim-fitting slacks, a silver-gray top and a purple-and-gray-striped jacket, she smiled as Lizzie pushed past her and dashed to his side.

"Are you okay, Pops?" she demanded after she'd grabbed his hand.

"I'm fine, sweetheart. Same as I was last time you were here. How about you?" His heart swelled as he scanned her pretty face. He couldn't have stopped his hand from lifting to brush across her dark hair if he'd wanted to. It was much neater than he'd ever managed.

Something inside him felt almost whole, complete, when Lizzie stared at him with her adoring gaze. Until he remembered he was responsible for her.

"Me an' Grace stayed on a real ranch! With horses," she breathed, her eyes wide in her round face. The usual listlessness vanished, until she added, "Kinda like our old one."

"You mean Miss Partridge," he corrected.

"I told Lizzie to call me Grace." His childhood friend pulled a chair forward and sat. She pushed an errant curl of her stunning hair off her face. "We can't stand on formality when we're living together."

"You live on a ranch? Then where we went wasn't…" Jack frowned.

"Oh, that's still my home. But I rented it out for a few months. Lizzie and I are staying at my friends' log cabin on their ranch. The Double H the locals call it," she explained so airily that he was immediately suspicious that she was hiding something. "It stands for Hanging Hearts Ranch. The house was empty anyway."

"You rented your house because you were leaving town?" The surprise on her face told Jack he'd guessed right. "So I've ruined your plans by coming here."

"Actually, you didn't. My friend Jess and I planned to take a trip together, but things came up. Your arrival just helped me act on an idea to send Jess in my place. The past year has been devastating for her. She needs a break."

"And you don't?" Aghast at what he'd caused, Jack leaned back and closed his eyes. *Why didn't You stop me, God? Why don't You ever help me when I need it?*

"I don't *need* a break because I'm not stressed out." Grace smiled when the door opened and a woman wearing jeans and a striped Western shirt entered. "Hello, dear. Jack, this is my friend, Mandy Calhoun. She's been kind enough to watch Lizzie several times."

"Nice to meet you, Mandy." Jack felt a flicker of envy at the way his granddaughter quickly moved beside the new arrival and took her hand. Then he figured it was pretty stupid of him to be jealous. He'd come here with the sole purpose of getting help for Lizzie, and these two women had done just that. "Thank you for helping Gracie."

Though the woman's eyebrows rose at his nickname, she merely said, "I'm glad I could be of some use. I hope you feel better soon." She turned to Grace. "I wondered if Lizzie would like to come with Ella and me for the rest of the afternoon."

"Saturday is your library afternoon, isn't it?" Grace's expression softened. "You always were a big reader, Mandy." Jack noticed she didn't ask his opinion but turned to Lizzie. "Would you like to go?"

"I already have a book," Lizzie said quietly as she wrapped her arms around her middle.

"You're almost finished it, aren't you? You could get another," Jack said.

"We're going to make cookies after library time," Mandy explained. "And then we'll play some games in the yard. It's beautiful out today."

"That sounds like a lot of fun, darlin'," Jack encouraged.

"But I wanna stay with you, Pops," she said, a frown marring her pretty face.

"Oh, we can't stay here all day," Grace told her.

"Why not?" Lizzie demanded.

"The doctors and nurses won't allow it. Your grandfather and the other patients need to rest so they can get better," Grace explained, her tone firm. "But perhaps you and I could come back later for a short visit."

Lizzie was staring at him as if questioning Gracie's comment. Jack nodded.

"I'd like that a lot, Sweet Pea. I'll be finished with my nap by then."

"You don't take naps, Pops," his granddaughter scoffed.

"The doctor said I do today." He forced a laugh. "Since I promised I'd do what he told me because I want to get out of here, I'm takin' a nap."

"You never did what anyone said a'fore." After a long pause in which Lizzie studied him suspiciously, she finally nodded. "Okay." She picked up the backpack she insisted on taking everywhere she went and gazed up at Mandy. "Where's Ella?"

"Her dad's bringing her. We're going to meet them for lunch. Hamburgers. Would you like to join us?"

"Yes, please." Lizzie licked her lips. "I love hamburgers."

"Me, too." Mandy waited until Lizzie hugged and kissed Jack. Then the two left with a wave.

"Sounds like she'll be having a ball," he said.

"Yes. And now we can continue our talk," Grace said, eyes narrowed as she focused on him. "If you're up to it."

"Sure," he agreed. He didn't want to talk about his past. There were too many things he was ashamed of, too many failures, too much pain. But he probably had to reveal more of his personal history because Gracie deserved to know the truth if she was going to take on him and Lizzie. "What do you want to know?"

"Start from when you left here," she ordered. She pulled a small bottle of water from her handbag. "Your parents?"

"They've passed."

"I'm sorry." Grace tilted her head sideways. "You left here for Dallas and…?" She leaned back, waiting.

"Shortly after we left, Dad and I had a big argument. Same as when we lived here, he kept insisting I work at the church, as a kind of pre-training for the ministry. He was adamant. I refused but he kept pushing and wouldn't listen to what I wanted. I couldn't take it anymore so eventually I ran away." Jack stopped, struggling not to relive that horrible feeling of being totally alone, unloved and uncared for. The desperate hopelessness of trying to please a taskmaster who seemed to despise his own son.

"Ran to where?" Grace asked calmly. Did nothing faze the woman?

"Mostly the streets in California. Got in trouble, got arrested. You've heard this story before." He shrugged. "The third time I was charged, the judge said he'd give me my last chance and warned me not to blow it. He sent me to his friend in Texas, a guy named Milt Sommers." Jack smiled in recollection of that first meeting. "Milt was a bachelor, a rancher, and he was tough as old boots. But he was also the fairest man I've ever known, even more stubborn than me. He put me to work, on his terms."

"You loved him," she said softly.

"Milt was a great guy." Why did everyone use that word *love* all the time? "He helped me figure out my life, taught me about horses and how to run the ranch. He taught me that your words had to match your deeds. When he died, he left me everything he owned." Jack swallowed the lump in his throat. Though Milt had been gone for years, the sense of deep personal loss remained.

"I'm so sorry," Grace murmured, her tone sympathetic.

"Thanks." Jack nodded. "It was hard to sell his Bar M, but I couldn't manage the spread and deal with Lizzie. Didn't really want to if I'm honest."

"Because?" Grace sat there waiting as if she had nothing else to do. Which meant she'd insist he told her all of it.

"Because everything reminded me of Cade," he told her harshly. *And Sheena and a bad marriage.* "Also, by then I'd figured out photography was my real passion. I'd put it aside, mostly because of Milt. He was so good to me." He smiled, remembering with fondness that gentle man who'd given unstintingly to Jack, to his community, to everyone, often without them even knowing. "I owed him to stick around and run the place when he no longer could."

"That was kind," Gracie murmured.

"I also felt I had a duty to Sheena." He'd certainly paid that bill. "And Cade, too." Jack shoved the memories back. "Cade was ten when Sheena died. He immediately dropped all the activities she'd enrolled him in. I didn't argue because I'd always thought he had too much on his plate anyway."

"Kids are often overloaded with activities," Grace agreed.

"I was a little surprised when he refused to consider college though. Academically he was very strong. But Cade insisted he wanted to ranch. Well, I sure wasn't going to argue with him like my father had with me," Jack said emphatically.

"Why would you?"

"Exactly. I taught him everything I'd learned from Milt." Now the memories were sweet. "We had some real good times, just the two of us, working together. Cade took to ranching like a duck to water and later, his wife was the same. They were crazy about animals."

"He married a woman who shared his interests. How lovely," Grace murmured.

"Celeste was his perfect partner." Jack's recollection of the couple made him smile even as he pushed away bitter reminders of his own marriage. "Those two newlyweds sure didn't need me hanging around, so I packed up my cameras and went traveling. They could have called anytime and I would have come back to help, but they weathered every storm together."

"You must have gone back to check on them?"

"Oh, yeah. I'd drop in now and then, especially after Lizzie arrived." He couldn't help but chuckle. Precious, special Lizzie. "I have a million pictures of that little girl."

"She is a cutie." Grace nodded.

"I returned more frequently after Lizzie's birth and stayed longer. Then one day Cade mentioned he and Celeste hadn't had a vacation since they'd been married. He asked if I'd run the ranch and care for Lizzie while they left for two weeks." Jack blocked the rush of emotion and said baldly, "They never came back."

He stopped, exhaled and tried to quash the rush of grief of two lives taken so needlessly, almost gagging at the memory of those black days. Always observant, Gracie rose, held his glass so he could take a sip, then set it on the table and returned to her seat. She said nothing for several moments, obviously digesting what he'd told her.

"And you never made up with your parents?" she asked softly.

"Oh, yeah. Milt insisted on that early on." Jack shrugged. "I guess by then Dad had finally realized I wasn't the type to minister to anyone. He said he forgave me before he died."

"Forgave you?" She frowned. "For what? Not wanting what he did?"

"I guess." Jack wasn't going there. "My sisters still live in the Dallas area, you know."

"Neither of them can take Lizzie?" she wondered aloud.

"They're both lots older than me, remember? Dinah has lung issues now," he explained. "Bethany has multiple sclerosis. A young kid like Lizzie would be too hard on them."

"Celeste's mom? Father?" Grace wondered.

"She was an only child. Her parents are in a nursing home. Early-onset Alzheimer's," he explained.

"Oh, how sad." He'd always liked the way Gracie showed such genuine remorse over the plights of others. "How have you managed since your son died?" She held his gaze, which told Jack he'd better not try to fudge the truth.

"I tried to keep ranching, mostly for Lizzie's sake." He hadn't wanted to stay there because every nook and cranny held awful memories, but he *had* tried. "It was her legacy, you know? From her parents."

"But you couldn't manage?"

"I didn't have enough time for her and ranching, and she was getting more and more withdrawn. She'd cling to me all the time and when I had to leave, she'd weep. Eventually she just withdrew into her own world. The sitters I paid to stay with her didn't help. Neither did the therapists." Jack shrugged as the same old helplessness overtook him. "I sold the place. We went to Boston for her to see a special therapist. Then we came here, to see you." Now it was his turn. "Will you marry me, Gracie? Help me raise Lizzie?"

"I don't think so," she admitted honestly. "But I haven't worked things through that far yet. It depends."

"On what?"

"You should rest now, Jack," she prevaricated.

Rest? How, when he'd made no progress in fulfilling his goal? He'd really hoped Gracie would agree to help. He remembered her as being so amenable.

"I'll rest a whole lot better when my granddaughter is taken care of," he growled, utterly exasperated that he couldn't pin Grace down. "She's taken to you like no one else. You're perfect for her. You can't refuse." He knew immediately that he'd said the wrong thing.

"Listen here, Jack Prinz. *You* waltzed into *my* world, laid this on me without any preparation, and expect me to drop everything and marry you? That isn't going to happen," she bristled, her pansy eyes darkening until they were almost black. "You just be quiet now and hear *me* out."

Her spirited response both startled and delighted Jack. *Sweet* Gracie Partridge indeed. He quickly covered his mouth, pretending a cough to hide his amusement. Best to hear her objections to marriage. Then he'd figure out how to counter them.

"Go ahead. I'm listening, Gracie," he invited.

"You're not being realistic," she snapped. "You can hardly expect that I would blankly agree to your scheme. But even if I did, I'd have a lot of questions and need more information and a lot more time to consider things from every viewpoint. And I'd need to pray about it."

Pray? Not exactly the response he wanted!

"But Lizzie needs your help now," he insisted.

"I'll do the best I can for her, Jack." Her eyes nailed him. "But here's my bottom line. If how I choose to deal with your request doesn't work for you, I think you'd better look elsewhere for help because I will *not* be rushed into marriage."

Grace rose, slid the strap of her bag over her shoulder and walked to the door. She had her hand on the knob before he realized she actually *intended* to walk out on him and found his voice.

"I'm sorry, Gracie." Relieved that she stopped, Jack cleared his throat and tried again. "I'm really sorry. I keep forgetting that even though I've been thinking about it for a while, this is all new to you. Please sit down. Ask me anything you like."

"My name is Grace," she said sternly. But she did return to her chair.

"Grace," he repeated obediently, hating that she'd broken the one tenuous connection he'd clung to from their past. "Okay. What do you want to know?"

"Lots of things. But not all at once. We can get to know each other slowly."

"But I want to get married right away," he blustered.

"*Not* going to happen," she warned in a soft but icy tone. "Deal with it."

Surprised by her obstinacy, Jack fell silent as he studied her, trying to decipher more about this woman who seemed nothing like the acquiescent girl he remembered.

"What you need to do now is take a step back. Relax, work on feeling better and stop trying to force me into your plans. Because it won't work." She shook her head when he tried to speak. "Listen to me, Jack. Lizzie and I will get to know each other better. That should be simple since we're living together. I promise I'll figure out ways to help her."

"But—" He glared at her, stymied and frustrated because he didn't know how to get through to this woman, couldn't find the way to motivate her to comply. "That's not what I planned."

"I realize that." Grace studied him intently. "But this is how it's going to be."

"Why?" he demanded.

"Because I barely know you after all these years and you certainly don't know me." Her eyes met his unflinchingly. "Also, I don't make major life decisions unless I know it's God's will for me. And I don't know that." Her gaze narrowed. "Have *you* prayed about it?"

"I've thought it over long and hard," he answered, dodging her question.

"Not what I mean." She sighed. "We must first work out if we can be friends. And right now, friendship is my only offer," she added quickly, before he could interrupt.

Jack might not have seen Gracie Partridge since they were teens, but he recognized the stubborn jut of her jaw. She'd made up her mind and she would follow her course. He could either agree or abandon the whole plan.

Abandonment might be the best course to take right now, but Jack wasn't going to do it. First and foremost, because he didn't have anyone else he could count on, and second, because despite their years apart, he knew beyond a shadow of a doubt that Grace was exactly who Lizzie needed. Nobody changed their personality that much. There had to be some of the old Gracie left inside. Proof of that was her insistence on waiting, on praying. Her faith had always been foremost in her life and he kind of liked that.

Third and perhaps most important, Jack hated being alone.

He'd wait because he had no other option. But while he waited, he'd figure out how to get through to her. Somehow. The idea of courting almost made him nauseous. All that kowtowing again? Sheena had expected expensive gifts she could show off, as if they were some kind of proof that he was worthy of her attention.

Gracie is not Sheena, his brain reminded.

"I do want to be friends again, Gracie— Grace," he corrected, stifling his impatience. "Just as we used to be." *Even though I can't love you.* "But I don't want Lizzie to keep suffering while we're working on getting along. I don't want to waste time."

"I do hope getting to know me better won't be a waste of time," she shot back, brows arched.

"I didn't mean…" *Shut up, Jack.*

"We'll have as much time as God gives us," she said briskly. "And that will be enough because He makes all things beautiful in His time."

"He certainly did with you." Jack gazed at her unabashedly, realizing in that moment that it wasn't just that Grace was a beautiful woman. It was something inside, something special that shone through and gave her that radiant glow that women around the world spent millions trying to achieve.

"Let's agree on the basics," she said, a slight flush coloring her cheeks as she dipped her head and dug in her bag for a tiny notebook and pen while she avoided meeting his gaze. "Lizzie and I are staying at Hanging Hearts Ranch for the next while."

She seemed slightly flustered, which Jack found reassuring. Maybe she wasn't quite as "in charge" as she seemed.

"What about school?" she asked.

"What school?" He blinked, mystified.

"Your granddaughter's. The school year has almost two months left. Where is Lizzie in her studies?" Grace asked.

"Before we left Boston, her teacher said missing the rest of the year was fine because she's way ahead so…" He shrugged.

"That's good, but I think it would be a good idea for Lizzie to attend class for the rest of the school year anyway. It will help her make friends and feel more comfortable when her year begins again in September. Agreed?"

When he nodded, Grace continued with her questions, writing his answers in the same tiny script that he recalled from high school. A nurse came in to check on him. Sometime after that, in the midst of Gracie's verbal notations about where he could stay when he was released, Jack began to nod off.

"You're tired. We'll continue some other time." Grace tucked away her notes and rose. "I'll be back with Lizzie later." She walked to the door.

"Gracie—Grace?" Jack waited until she was looking at him. "Thank you."

"Don't thank me yet. I've never been a mother or grandmother and I'm not at all sure I'll be very good at it," she informed him in a crisp tone.

"I am. I'm absolutely positive you'll be perfect." He smiled at her uplifted brow. "Can you leave your cell phone number so I can call you if anything changes?"

"Yes, of course." She wrote it on a piece of paper and tucked it under his water glass.

"I think we're going to be good friends, Gra—ce," he assured her, correcting himself midsentence. "We were once," he reminded her.

"Yes, we were," she agreed very quietly, her forehead pleated in a sober expression. "But that was a long time ago and a lot has changed. Rest now, Jack."

The warmth of her presence left with her.

Now alone, Jack squinted out the window, his brain replaying what Grace had said. All things considered, it wasn't a bad start. She hadn't said she'd *never* marry him. He was good at talking people around to his side. Once he felt a little less like a punching bag, he'd coax Gracie to adopt his plan.

He leaned back and closed his eyes. But he couldn't rest. Not yet. It felt like he should *do* something.

Then it hit him. Maybe he couldn't persuade Gracie to marry him right away. But he could still make sure all his bases were covered. He grabbed his phone and hit Speed Dial.

"You know that report I ordered?" he said.

"Yeah. You said you didn't need to see it."

"Changed my mind. Send it now, will you? Thanks." Jack hung up and accessed his email, reading and rereading the investigator's report on Miss Grace Partridge, the one he'd commissioned when he'd first considered asking her to help Lizzie.

After scanning the document twice, he found no surprises. Gracie would be the perfect partner to help with Lizzie. Satisfied that he was in control of as much as he could be for now, Jack was finally able to relax.

Gracie was all about praying for direction, which he truly admired.

But after all, God helped those who helped themselves.

Chapter Three

"Is Pops gonna be in the hospital forever?" Lizzie's nonstop questions had been amusing at first, but Grace would welcome a break.

"They will probably release him today. If so, you and I will pick him up after school." She turned into the parking lot and pulled into a vacant spot. "Let's go meet your teacher and the other students now."

"What if I don't like it?" the little girl demanded with a glower.

"You will, dear. Just wait." Grace drew her alongside as they walked, chatting merrily about the school to forestall more questions about Jack, for which she had no answers.

She had deliberately handled Lizzie's registration while the child was in her room, hoping to spare the girl worry. After speaking with Anita McAllister, Grace was certain that years as Sunshine's kindergarten teacher had rendered the woman an expert at allaying childish apprehensions. That teacher hurried toward them now, her smile bright and welcoming.

"Hello, Grace. Come on in, Lizzie," Anita encouraged. "There are some children who would like to get to know you."

"Why?" Lizzie's topaz eyes narrowed suspiciously.

"Because you're new and you've been to places that they've never seen," the teacher answered calmly. "It's always nice to meet new people, don't you think?"

"I guess." Lizzie hugged her backpack and shrugged her disinterest.

For Grace, the shrug was reminiscent of Jack and that annoyed her. Why did the man keep invading her mind?

Grace waited to leave until they were in the classroom and Lizzie was surrounded by a group of girls, all asking questions.

"I'll pick you up after school, dear," she whispered.

"And then we'll go see Pops?" Lizzie waited for her nod before heaving a resigned sigh. Her smile reappeared when someone admired her T-shirt and within seconds she was engaged with her classmates.

Grace smiled at Anita and slipped away. As she entered her car, her sigh was much deeper than Lizzie's had been. The decision to stay here was the right one, but it hadn't resulted in any clarity from God about her future. She still felt like a cork floating on an ocean of uncertainty. What did He want her to do now? Or was she to be put out to pasture, no longer of any use to her Lord?

She drove to the local coffee shop, ordered her favorite cinnamon latte, and found a seat outside, in the warm sunshine, as she waited for the call Jess's early morning text had promised.

"How are you, dear?" Grace asked after answering the phone.

"Shocked, amazed, thrilled." Her friend laughed gaily. "I'm sitting by the pool with my coffee, a lovely fruity drink, and waffles with fresh strawberries and whipped cream, waiting to depart San Diego Harbor. Oh, Grace, this ship is just as wonderful as we thought it would be and you packed all the right things for this trip. But I'm so sad you're not here with me."

"Don't be." Grace quelled a frisson of envy. "I think I'm where God wants me, for now, though I miss your perspective."

"Well, I'm here now so ask away." Jess listened attentively as Grace laid out all that had happened since her departure. "Jack asked you to marry him again? That's so romantic," she breathed when Grace had finished.

"It's not romantic at all!" Grace cut across Jess's comment scornfully. "It's exasperating to have someone you knew from way back when show up on your doorstep and demand you to fall in with their plans immediately, completely disregarding the fact that in the thirty-odd years they've been gone you've made a life for yourself! It's just that I'm uncertain where to go from here."

"But he was your true love!"

"Jack Prinz was a teenage crush," Grace corrected. "I am not a teenager anymore."

"Well, you're not dead yet either." When Grace only huffed her annoyance, Jess sighed. "I knew I shouldn't have left. I should be there for you."

"Of course you should have left." *Don't ruin her trip!* Grace quickly regrouped. "What could you do about Jack if you were here? He's just the same as he was then, bullishly determined to have his own way." She caught herself, sipped her latte and changed tactics. "I want you to enjoy yourself on this trip, Jess. I have no business dumping all over you and spoiling things."

"You haven't spoiled anything. You're my best friend. I want you to share whatever's happening in your world." That bracing tone helped soothe Grace's frustration. "So Jack's in the hospital and the child is in school. What do you *want* to happen next? You could move into my place if that would help," she offered.

"That's kind of you, dear, but I think I prefer the ranch right now." Grace explained her choice. "There's lots of help if I need it because the Calhouns and their families are all nearby. I'm also hoping their children will draw out Lizzie." She paused, then admitted, "Once school is over, I'm fairly certain I will need those kids to keep her busy. Lizzie's a lovely child, but she asks so many questions."

"And Jack?" Jess sounded tentative, as if she was afraid to hear the answer.

"Well, he's not happy that I nixed the whole marriage thing."

"Oh, no." Jess sounded disappointed. "Why did you do that, Grace?"

The question seemed ridiculous.

"Jess! A few Christmas-card scribbles are not a precursor to marriage. I barely know Jack now. I need time to consider all the ramifications of taking such a huge step without love. Just marrying him because he wants it doesn't feel right. And I don't have the inner assurance from God that I need before embarking on such a major change." She exhaled heavily. "I have a ton of reasons why such a thing wouldn't work."

"I'm hearing that," Jess murmured, sounding amused.

"I don't see the need to marry so hastily."

"It is your decision, but Lizzie is blessed to have you. So is Jack." The way Jess's voice trailed away meant she wasn't saying something.

"And?" Grace prodded.

"Well, I'm suddenly wondering if such a marriage would be enough for you." Jess paused. "I mean, from what you've told me, Jack hasn't said anything about caring for you, wishing you could have been together way back when?"

"No. He hasn't said that." Grace glanced at the happy couple sitting at a table across the way and wished she could recapture the carefree joy in life that these two exhibited. Jack's arrival had made her confusing world even more complicated.

"But you want him to, right?" Jess hinted.

"I think the best I can do is try to help Lizzie and trust that if it's God's plan for me to marry Jack, He'll work it all out. Don't you think?" she asked wistfully, unable to recall the last time she'd felt so uncertain about her future.

"Absolutely. The only certainty in this situation is your trust in God. Cling to that, Grace. Oh, just a minute." Jess said something to someone, then came back on the line. "I have to hang up now, dear. They're going to have another mandatory fire drill in ten minutes. I must finish my breakfast and then find my spot. But I will call you tomorrow."

"No, don't do that," Grace refused. "You'll be at sea, on your way to the Panama Canal. Find a deck chair and bask in the sun. Read a book. Enjoy! I'll be just fine," she added, hoping she was speaking truth.

"You *are* fine, girlfriend. Never doubt God *is* watching out for you. I will be praying for all three of you. Bye now," Jess said.

Grace hung up but didn't move for several moments. *Would* she be fine?

Trusting God with everything in her world

had started when she was a young girl. It had never been difficult—well, except for the heartache she'd had to overcome while learning to relinquish her dream of love, marriage and children. But that had been an ongoing process that had happened over a period of time. And it was over now.

This was different.

Jack's odd proposal felt as if he'd peeked into her very soul, found the tiny flicker of longing for a family she'd never had and fanned it back to life. But she wanted it doused! She didn't want to go through that whole process of grieving and letting go of that dream again.

Still, if Grace had learned one thing in all these years, it was that the only way to happiness was by standing firm on her trust in her Heavenly Father. God had known all about Jack and Lizzie. He'd known she would cancel her trip in order to help with Jack's bereaved granddaughter. If He had a special purpose for her in this situation, He'd give her the strength to do it.

Jack would just have to be patient while she figured things out.

Jack had never learned patience. And he didn't intend to start now.

That was another of his ongoing issues with God. Why give folks brains and the means to do things if you didn't expect them to go ahead and use them? Like now, for instance. He didn't need to wait for God to reveal the next step to him. He already knew he was being discharged and if he knew where he'd be going, he'd call a cab and get out of this hospital!

Problem was, in her phone call this morning, Gracie hadn't told him much about the new digs she said she was arranging. Now he was stuck waiting for her. Maybe he needed to pray about that. As if. Too many years had passed since he and God had conversed.

Where was the woman? Jack had been waiting all afternoon for her to appear. Restless and in ill humor, he did another tour of the hallway, just to prove to anyone who wanted to question him that his head injury and his ability with crutches would cause no further problems. He kept his expression blank. He sure wasn't going to tell the nosy nurses how much pain he was in. They might suggest more tests. His irritability rose.

When Jack returned to his room, Gracie was sitting there, waiting calmly, a cellophane-wrapped bouquet of pretty spring flowers at her feet.

"Not yours," she said, catching his glance. "They're for me."

"Where have you been? I've been ready to go for ages," Jack snapped as he eased onto the side of the bed, hoping the pain would decrease. "Where's Lizzie?"

"You can't leave here until the doctor discharges you." Grace looked stunning in a white sleeveless dress with teal sandals and a matching leather bag. She wore lapis earrings like those he'd brought home from the South Pacific for Cade's wife. "Mandy is bringing Lizzie here from school. Here's Dr. Fritz."

"Hello, Miss Partridge. One last examination of this patient and then you can take him away." The doctor checked Jack's pupils, lungs and heart rate. "Head injuries are not to be trifled with, sir. Don't overdo," he warned in a severe tone.

"I won't." Jack didn't like explaining himself to anyone, but given the man's excellent treatment of him, he felt compelled to stop the censure. "But I have to get out of here so I can care for my granddaughter."

"Passing out with only a child to help you isn't smart." Dr. Fritz glared at him. "And you sure can't take care of a child with your foot disabled."

"I'm—"

"Happily, I understand our Grace is available. You couldn't leave your granddaughter in better hands than hers. I'd think that you, apparently being an old friend of hers, should know that," Dr. Fritz scolded, one eyebrow arched.

"Of course I know it. But it's not fair to dump Lizzie—" Jack gave up when the man tsk-tsked his disapproval.

"Let Grace handle the child," the doctor ordered. "Be sure you don't try to cover up if you have any dizziness or blurry vision. Or any of the other things the nurse warned you about, including putting too much strain on that leg and foot. It's a matter of monitoring now."

"Thank you—" Jack stopped because the doctor had moved on.

"Grace, you're looking very beautiful, but I thought you were leaving us for three months?" Dr. Fritz had to be at least fifteen years older than Gracie, but he was gawking at her in a most admiring way.

"I was." Gracie shrugged, her smile as calm and unruffled as ever. "Plans change."

"Such a grand voyage." Fritz shook his head. "Altering that must have been difficult, especially when you've been anticipating it for so long."

Jack's curiosity was pricked. Gracie had mentioned leaving but he hadn't fully realized how completely he was interrupting her life. He grimaced. By coming here he'd probably ruined her vacation of a lifetime. This wasn't the way he'd thought things would go. Not at all.

Maybe coming here to coax Grace's help wasn't the genius plan he'd thought. Maybe too many years had gone by, too many changes. He wasn't the same person as he'd been, and he was beginning to realize she wasn't either. He heaved a weary sigh. It had all seemed so simple from the perspective of Boston.

"Perhaps I'll go a little later in the year," she said noncommittally.

"Huh." Dr. Fritz studied her a little longer before he fixed Jack with a dark look. "If Grace Partridge is in control, you have nothing to worry about. She's one of the most competent people I know. Your granddaughter is in good hands." He nodded and left.

"Does everyone around here sing your praises?" Jack asked crankily. He wished he hadn't when her eyes widened with hurt and her head drooped.

"Not everyone," she whispered very softly. "Some laugh at me."

"What?" He was aghast. "Why?"

"Oh, you know." She glanced at him then looked away. "I'm the silly old spinster librarian," she said quietly, and then added, "Who doesn't have a life."

"You're kidding, right?" Her reproachful glare made him pause. "Whoever said that needs their head examined. Silly? Old? Hardly. Look in the mirror, Gracie. You're beautiful. And as for spinster?" He snorted his disgust. "Haven't you heard? Staying single is the choice of the majority these days."

Jack would have said more, lots more if it would have erased the pain he'd glimpsed in Gracie's lovely eyes. But just then Lizzie walked in with Mandy. Relief filled her little face when she saw him dressed.

"We're leaving, right, Pops?" she asked quietly when she was standing next to him. Her hand found his and cuddled into it.

"Yes, we are. Thank you, Mandy," he said.

"You're very welcome." She smiled and waved. "I have to run some errands. See you at the Double H." She left.

"Are you okay, Pops?" Worry laced Lizzie's question.

"I am fine as frog's hair." He said it deliberately.

"Hey, that's what she says." Lizzie glanced at Gracie.

"I know. She got it from her dad. He used to say it all the time." Jack grinned at his old friend, relaxing just a little when she smiled back, her earlier dejection gone. "Your dad had lots of weird sayings, didn't he, Gracie—Grace?"

"Dad spoke very little English when we moved here. The more he learned, the more he mixed his idioms." She smiled fondly. "He made everyone laugh, but not all of his mistakes were accidental. He liked seeing people laugh."

"I remember something about not crying over spilled milk." Jack remembered the saying, but he pretended not to, just to hear Gracie clarify. "Only it didn't go quite like that."

"Don't cry over cracked diamonds, *mója droga*," she corrected, exactly as he'd expected. "No point because it's too late and the diamond is ruined." She chuckled at Jack's eye roll then shrugged. "He was a jeweler, after all."

"Are you coming to our log cabin today, Pops?" Lizzie asked very quietly.

"Uh, I don't know." He looked to Grace for help. Where would he stay?

"Your pops isn't staying at the log cabin, Lizzie. That's where you and I stay," Grace explained. "Besides, it has steps and the doctor says your pops can't climb them."

"Where *is* Pops gonna stay?" the child asked with a frown. "'Cause I wanna stay with him."

"Oh, he's staying at the ranch, too. You'll see him all the time," she promised, then faced Jack. "My friends Bonnie and Ben who own Hanging Hearts Ranch have offered you a room at the main house. No stairs." Grace smiled. "If that's okay?"

"Very kind of them." Jack saw the food trolley roll past his door and gulped. No way did he want to force down another bowl of that awful soup. "Can we leave now?" he asked hurriedly. "I hate hospitals."

Grace cleared her throat. When she had his attention, she nodded toward Lizzie, who was watching him with wide eyes.

"Not exactly hate," he quickly corrected. "But I'm better so I don't need to be here."

"Then we'll go." Grace picked up her flowers. "Shall we?"

"Yes!" He grabbed his crutches and thumped behind her out of the room, wondering where she found such elegant and flattering clothes. Beside her he felt like a country bumpkin with his tattered jeans and dirty shirt. He should have asked her to bring him some clean stuff from the suitcase in his car. But what did it matter? Nothing he owned looked half as swank as what she was wearing.

While they waited for the elevator, Jack leaned against the wall to catch his breath.

"I'm sorry. Was I moving too fast?" Grace studied him in that perceptive all-knowing way she had. "It must be frustrating for you to feel so weak."

"I am not weak!" As if!

"Pops." Lizzie glared at him with disapproval. "You shouldn't yell. Grace says you gotta be quiet in a hospital so the sick people can rest."

"I— Sorry, honey." This is what it had come to? His own granddaughter chewing him out for bad behavior? Jack exhaled and stepped into the elevator, bumping his foot as he tried to maneuver his crutches. Pain shot up his leg. About to utter an expletive, he caught Gracie's eye and swallowed it, suffering in silence until they arrived in the lobby.

"Do you want to sit down while I get the car?" Grace asked. "Maybe you need to rest—"

"I'm fine." He took great care *not* to lean against the wall. "Lizzie will stay, too."

"But—" His granddaughter abruptly stopped arguing. Jack wondered why until he caught the merest shake of Grace's head. "I'll stay with Pops," she agreed quietly.

"Good. I won't be long." Grace hurried away.

"How come you're mad, Pops?" Lizzie demanded. "Did I do sumthin' bad?"

"No." Jack forced a smile. "And I'm not mad."

Lizzie stared at him reproachfully for several minutes.

"What?" he finally asked.

"Grace says God doesn't want us to lie." She tipped her head to one side.

"Do you like Grace?" he asked, needing to change the subject, fast.

"Yes. She's nice. She knows *everybody*." Lizzie seemed amazed by that. Then she frowned. "She said I had to go to school until it was over. Did she tell you?"

"We talked about it. I think it's a good idea," Jack said, knowing very well that to differ from Grace would only harm the new relationship his granddaughter was beginning to build with her. "You've been there. Did you like it?"

"It was okay. The teacher reads us really good stories. I like stories," she said, staring into the distance.

"I know." He smiled. "You're like your dad. He loved books, too. Do you remember?"

"No." Lizzie tilted her head to frown at him. "I forget about them all the time," she said sadly. "How come I forget, Pops?"

"Everyone does. As time passes, we all forget little things about people we've lost," he explained as gently as he could. "But we never forget the important things. We keep those tucked in our hearts to remember."

"What are the important things to remember?"

When Sheena died, Jack hadn't wanted to remember anything. Not the way he'd been hoodwinked, not the way she'd always made him the bad guy with Cade, not the many times she'd told him she hated him but refused to divorce him because of Milt's money.

"Pops?" When he didn't immediately answer, Lizzie's fingers threaded through his. She looked at him with such a beseeching gaze that he had to swallow his painful past to concentrate and find a few examples for this grief-filled child.

"Memories like how your mom hugged you so tight," he managed to say, gulping past the lump in his throat as he dredged up memories of the few happy years he'd shared with his son and his family. "And how your daddy used to swing you up in the saddle so you could ride Pixie." Jack deliberately mentioned her pony, hoping she'd ask about riding again.

But Lizzie was off on another tangent.

"And how he used to swing me round and round. It made me laugh so hard." She giggled to herself, hugging her arms around her middle.

Lizzie continued with her memories but Jack didn't hear them because Grace drove up—in *his* brand-new luxury model SUV. The one he'd hankered after for years. The one he'd sold his truck for and splurged on only *after* they'd disembarked from the plane in Missoula to come and see Gracie. The one he'd hoped to impress her with.

The one she was now *driving*! Jack couldn't breathe. His back teeth crushed together as his fancy new tires scuffed the curb, sounding as bad to him as fingernails scraping on a blackboard.

"You have a nice car, Jack," Grace complimented him. "Though it's not as responsive as I'd expected." She looked askance at the vehicle for a moment before hurrying to open the passenger door for him. "What's wrong? Do you need help to get in?" she added in a whisper when he didn't move.

"No," he managed to mutter. "Thanks."

He wanted to tell her he'd drive his new car, but the crutches reminded him that was impossible. By the time he'd maneuvered himself and them into the vehicle, Lizzie was already belted into her car seat in the back.

"All right then. Here we go." Grace got into

the driver's seat and touched the start button. The engine roared.

So did Jack. But silently.

"Don't push the gas," he ordered when he found his voice.

"But to start it—"

"You don't have to touch the gas to start it," he repeated more forcefully.

"Well, I did before," she told him in a pert tone he understood to mean he should be quiet. Then she frowned. "Maybe I should have brought my car."

Yeah, maybe.

"Why didn't you?" Jack asked.

"It would be tougher for you to get into, especially with your cast and those crutches." Grace shifted into Drive and they slowly rolled forward. "I'm guessing this is hard on gas," she speculated as she drove. "But it doesn't seem to have the zip my car does."

Jack wasn't going to dignify that with a response because Grace probably didn't know much about vehicles.

"I'll tell you about Hanging Hearts Ranch," she said as she cruised through Sunshine at half the posted speed. "Bonnie and Ben Halston run it. The three Calhoun boys are their adopted sons and they all work on the ranch in some capacity or other. The ranch holds a lot of guest events but it's not terribly busy right now because it's not quite their tourist season. It's still a bustling place with their big herds though. I think you'll like it there."

"It will be fine. Until we get married," he added, sneaking a look at her expression.

"Jack! You are not to say that. To anyone." Grace's firm tone held a warning. "Nor you either, Lizzie."

"Okay," Lizzie agreed happily. "Why not?"

"Because I have not agreed to get married and I do not want the entire town speculating about it while I make up my mind. Do you understand?"

"Uh-huh." Lizzie shrugged and pulled a book out of her ever-present backpack.

"Jack?"

He didn't agree.

"I want to get this done, Grace. I don't want to dally around, putting in time—"

"There is no debate. Either you agree to keep silent or I'll stop here and you and your fancy car can leave." Grace hit the brakes so hard, Jack had to grab the dash to stop from hitting his head. "Well?"

Lizzie gave a grunt at the abrupt jerk but immediately went back to her story. Maybe because she knew he was determined to marry this woman no matter how hard she made it for him.

"We can't sit here all day, Grace," he warned, worried someone might come up behind them and bump into his precious vehicle. "We'll talk about it later," he said, hoping to mollify her.

"We'll talk about it now and I will have your promise, or *we* won't be going to the Double H." She kept her hands on the wheel, but those purple-almost-black eyes nailed him in place. "Well?"

"Fine. We'll keep it between us. For now." Thus defeated, Jack inclined his head to the side and tried to relax enough that its throbbing would ease off. No way he was going to admit it, but he wanted to lie down. Badly.

"Thank you." Grace moved back onto the road and took a right turn. "I'll introduce you to Bonnie and Ben and make sure you're settled in, but then I'm going to have to leave."

"What?" He gasped. "I don't even know these people, Grace."

"You'll get to know them very quickly. And I will be there. Just not right away," she asserted. This Grace was so *not* the malleable girl Jack had known.

"What's so urgent?" he demanded.

"Mandy managed to squeeze me in for a riding lesson," she said, turning off the highway and under a black metal sign that proclaimed this Hanging Hearts Ranch. "I'm learning English riding."

"English?" He stared at her.

"Dressage. I usually have a lesson every week. I'd canceled my weekly morning spot when I thought I'd be away, but Mandy was able to fit me in today." She sighed. "I just love riding. Last year Mandy taught me to do some tricks."

Jack couldn't speak. Not only was he silenced by the mental image of Grace Partridge riding a trick horse, he was more shocked that she enjoyed it.

"When— ?" He cleared his throat to get rid of the squeak and lowered his voice. "When did you learn to ride?"

"I guess it's been four or five years now," she said. "Before I retired, I decided my life had become boring and that I needed to challenge myself."

"By trick riding." Jack stared at her through new eyes. "What other hobbies do you have? Skateboarding? Skydiving?"

"Good grief, no. Though I did try kite surfing on the snow last winter." She chuckled. "It was great fun, but it was quite difficult for me to control the sail when the wind blew hard so I gave that up."

He was almost afraid to ask, but his curiosity won out.

"Gave it up for what?"

"Oh, I've tried several things since. Even calf roping." Her nose wrinkled and she shook her head. "That wasn't much fun for me. I felt sorry for the calf. But it's a big deal around here. In fact, Bonnie and Ben are hoping to organize a kids' rodeo with calf roping. I'm sure they'll tell you all about it if you ask. Here we are."

Jack studied the big, sprawling ranch house that looked very similar to the one he'd called home in Texas.

When he'd arrived at Gracie's house, staying on a ranch with strangers was not what he'd expected. But then, neither was a broken leg or a rejection of his proposal. Maybe Grace was right. Maybe they did need some time to get to know each other again.

"Lizzie and I stay in that little log cabin," she said, pointing to it. "It won't be too far, will it? Just across the yard?"

"I can't do the stairs. But I guess we could meet at the table in front." Jack fell silent, thinking about how little he really knew about Grace.

"Are you sure it's okay?" she murmured softly. Her careful tone told him she was worried. "Sunshine is such a small town that there are few places to rent. I thought this was a good solution, but if—"

"It will be great. Thank you for helping us out," Jack said quietly. "We aren't your problem, Grace. It's kind of you to settle things for us."

"Oh, good." That smile of hers was worth a lot of inconvenience. "Now here come Bonnie and Ben, so let's get you to your room. You might want to rest a bit. They've invited us to share tonight's meal with them."

"Sounds great." Actually, it did. Jack was more than willing to fall in with Grace's plan if it meant she'd be a little more amenable to *his* plan. But somewhere along the way he'd need to ensure she knew marriage to him didn't include love. He'd learned that lesson well, and he had no desire to retake the tests.

Jack eased his aching body out of the car while he ordered his mind to come up with a new way to impress Grace. Crutches and weakness were hardly going to create the impression he wanted.

Time to regroup.

Chapter Four

"That was a very fine dinner, Bonnie. Thank you."

Grace watched Jack set his empty coffee cup on the table and beam his most charming smile. As she'd expected, Bonnie blushed. Well, what woman wouldn't? It wasn't Jack's fault that he'd been born a charmer.

"And, Ben." He scanned his host's face with a grin. "I sure appreciate you and your boys telling me about your plans for that kids' rodeo."

So gallant. Grace hid her smile and waited. She may not have seen Jack for years, but that familiar gleam in his eyes told her he hoped for an invitation to join in planning the rodeo. She had no doubt he'd get it. The only question was how long it would take.

"You mentioned you used to hold kids' rodeos on your ranch, Jack," Ben said. "We'd like to hear more about that, when you're rested up and want to talk some more, of course."

"What Dad's not saying is that for years we've offered trail rides for kids, taken them to the hills to explore the caves, hiked old and young pretty well all over this ranch," Drew told him with a chuckle.

"Not to mention the campfires and sing-alongs,

chuck wagon eat-outs, riding lessons, hayrides, sleepovers in the wild—you name it, we've done it," Zac added.

"But we've never held a rodeo for kids," Sam joined in. "And we want this one to be extra special so we can raise a nice chunk of money."

"Uh-huh." The thoughtful way Jack scratched his chin was pure drama. If he stayed, Grace was going to rope him into joining Sunshine's theater group. "This money," he paused for effect, continuing only when he held everyone's attention. "You said it's for a kids' summer camp?"

"Yes." Ben nodded. "The place has been around for years, but it's getting really tired and worn. It's a nonprofit so they don't take in a lot with their summer fees. We'd like to raise enough for them to do a few repairs, painting for one. A couple of roofing jobs. Maybe some updates on the leaders' quarters. That kind of thing."

"That's a real nice idea. I'd love to help. I'll start thinking on it and make a list." Jack held up his hands as if to protest. "Not that you have to do what we did," he blustered as he struggled to rise. "Just ideas, that's all I'll have to offer."

Ha! Grace knew Jack would be running the show before too long. That's who he'd always been, a leader. And she was glad. As part of the rodeo committee she would welcome fresh new ideas.

"Now, after such an amazing meal, I'll give Bonnie a hand with these dishes. Oops!" He overbalanced awkwardly but quickly recovered. "After that, I better walk around a bit to get the wiggles out of my legs."

Everyone laughed. Lizzie giggled and made a joke.

"You're our guest, Jack," Sam protested as he lifted the plate from Jack's hands. "We Calhoun boys took over doing dishes the first day Bonnie and Ben brought us to the Double H. If our wives were here and not in town signing our kids up for summer sports, they could testify that we haven't lost our skills in that department."

"Yeah, go ahead for your walk, Jack," Zac agreed. "I'm thinking that cast must be itching a bit from the way you've been fidgeting. Maybe some exercise will help."

"Thought I was hiding it. You're sure?" At their insistence Jack shrugged. "Okay. You're the doctor, Zac." After excusing himself he hobbled on his crutches toward the door. "Want to come along?" he asked in a quiet voice as he passed Grace's chair.

"I suppose." Grace rose. She followed him outside only after she heard Lizzie ask Bonnie if she'd play a song on the piano. Once she and Jack were well clear of the main house and all possibility of anyone overhearing them, she added, "I'll come, as long as you stop playing cowboy."

"Gracie, darlin', I *am* a cowboy," he said with a grin. "Have been for some years."

"Uh-huh. You're planning to stick around here all summer?" she asked, just to clarify. "Long enough to see the rodeo through?"

"Long enough to make you Mrs. Jack Prinz," he shot back with an outrageous wink.

"That's yet to be decided. And just so you know, I don't intend to move from Sunshine. It's my home and I'm staying right here."

"Fine by me," he said amicably. "I always liked the town. Your place especially. Just say when, darlin'."

"It's not that easy," Grace protested. Annoyed by his easy acquiescence and the reminder of how often he'd hung out at her family home in the past, she frowned at the sky. "I'm not getting a strong response from God on that subject and I need one before I can decide."

"Maybe He doesn't care," Jack said with a shrug.

"Yes, He does." She glared at him.

"Whatever. You know, back there," he jerked his head toward the house, "I realized something. Except for the fancy clothes and that pretty hair, you haven't changed much, Gracie." He tilted his head to one side as he studied her. "Not the inside of you, leastways. You always were gracious and kind. And you always had a strong faith in God. Far stronger than mine, and *I* was the preacher's kid."

"I doubt my faith was stronger than yours," she demurred. "But back then I think you equated your relationship with God to the one you had with your father, which did neither of them any benefit."

Because she was fairly certain the deepening lines at the corner of his lips were due to pain, she deliberately chose to sit on one of the amazing log benches that Ben had made. They were scattered around the Double H so you could rest at a multitude of different sites and still savor an amazing view.

She wanted to say more about Jack's relationship with his father, but struggled to find the right way to express herself. Hopefully, he wouldn't become offended if she was totally honest with him.

"You don't have to tiptoe around me, girl," Jack said as if he guessed the reason for her hesitation. "Say what's on your mind."

"All right, I will." Grace exhaled and dove in. "I always wondered if your dad's constant desire to find a bigger church was because he somehow felt inadequate to the task of ministry, like maybe he believed a larger church would bring coworkers or perhaps other pastors with whom he could confer, sound out his ideas and find support."

"Shortly before he died, he told me exactly that." Jack blinked his surprise. "How did you know?"

"I didn't *know*. It was just a hunch. People always have a reason for their actions." She shrugged. "Perhaps that's why he was so desperate for you to get into the ministry, too. Because he needed, wanted you to support him."

"Maybe." Jack thought about it a while before saying, "Dad never explained why he pushed so hard. All I know is that he was always ordering me to plan for seminary, and when I refused, telling me how useless my life was. Dad and I never talked about God much even when I lived with Milt, after I went to visit him."

"Why not?" Grace asked.

"What does it matter?" he growled.

Grace kept silent. She knew Jack didn't want to get into a discussion about God, but she had a feeling that if she kept talking to him about it, they might somehow bridge the faith distance that yawned between them.

"I loved my dad, but he never loved me, Gracie," Jack admitted in a strangled voice.

"Oh, I'm sure you're wrong." She was appalled, both by his words and by the pain she could hear underlying them.

"I'm not wrong," he insisted. "I grew up knowing it. Even though I kept hoping he'd find something in me to care about, that never happened. It's one reason I ran away from home. I couldn't live like that anymore."

The anguish in his words hurt to hear. Grace reached out to touch his hand, to support him.

"Maybe your father didn't know how to show love?" she suggested very softly.

"He never had that trouble with my sisters," Jack said bitterly. "I was the one who was unlovable." As if he needed the contact, he wrapped his fingers around her hand and held it tightly between them.

"Jack, I—"

"I don't want to talk about it anymore. It's over. At least he didn't die with hate between us." Jack hurried on. "I guess the point I was trying to make is that Dad quit harping at me, probably because he finally figured out that God and I didn't get along either."

"What you really mean is that God won't do what you want Him to," she simplified with a smile. "Right?"

"Maybe," he admitted. "Call it what you like, Gracie, but I've never understood what God wants from me. As a kid, I tried to do all the things my parents told me to do to get close to God. I prayed, I read my Bible, I did good deeds."

"But that all seemed pointless," she added, nodding. "Of course it did."

"Why *of course*?" His frown revealed his confusion. Or maybe he didn't like it when she tugged her hand from his.

"Because God doesn't want duty worship or rote prayers." Sadness that Jack hadn't yet found faith and a strong trust in his Heavenly Father swamped her. But then, Grace had her own trust issues. Like why didn't He respond to her prayer for guidance?

"Gracie? Why have you gone so quiet?"

"Just sorting through some things," she said

hurriedly, not wanting him to start guessing at her thoughts. "God is a personal God, Jack. He wants a personal relationship with His children that they *want* to have with Him."

"Guess I never felt like I mattered that much to Him, that I didn't measure up to His expectations, just like I never mattered to Dad when I wouldn't do what he wanted." Jack's words reeked of bitterness. "The way he preached, God was a taskmaster who demanded obedience and subservience, and if He didn't get it, I was damned."

"Are you sure your dad actually preached that? Or is that what *you* told yourself?" Grace didn't wait for his response. "Because as I age, I'm realizing that a lot of things I have long believed to be true actually aren't. They're mostly made up of partial memories, impressions and my own viewpoints."

"Got an example?" His expression revealed his curiosity.

"My past, for one," Grace said. "You know my parents and I moved from Poland to Sunshine when I was three. Or so I thought. As a kid, I remember Mom and Dad talking about the journey over on a ship." She smiled. "I thought *I* remembered the waves and how a particular man on the ship smelled of sausage."

"What does that mean? That everything I knew about you was wrong." Jack frowned, obviously confused. "You're *not* from Poland?"

"Yes, originally. But I was only six months old when my parents emigrated." She smiled at his surprise. "I couldn't have remembered the waves, not at that early age."

"Okay." Jack kept studying her while he waited for her to continue.

"The sausage smell that I think I remember was most likely from a time after we left the ship. The reason I believe that is because I only recently learned about a neighbor who lived next door to us in Billings. He was a Polish sausage maker." She shook her head and grimaced. "I didn't even know we'd lived in that city! I thought we'd come straight off the ship to Sunshine."

"Well, that's a small detail that a young child could easily forget," Jack murmured.

"Not the point," she chided.

"What is then?" He arched one eyebrow in that imperious manner of his. He wasn't pretending confusion. Jack truly didn't understand what she was getting at.

"The point is, I was so certain my memories were accurate that I had never questioned them." She lifted her hands, palms up. "I *knew* that I'd lived here all my life. I *thought* I knew everything about my past."

"And this proves you don't know your past?" He looked at her skeptically.

"I don't know. Not by a long shot," she asserted. "When I was clearing out my parents' things, I found my mother's diaries. That was an eye-opener because I had misremembered a lot." How had Jack remained so handsome? *Focus, Grace.* "What I'm saying is, maybe it was the same thing with you and your father. Maybe you remembered inaccurately."

"Maybe." Judging by his eye roll, Jack doubted it, though he didn't say so.

"It's not just my family's history," she continued. "Remember the church camp we went to?"

"Ben talking about raising money for his camp reminded me of it," he replied. "I'd like to go see it sometime."

"You saw it years ago. It's the same one, Jack." She laughed at his disbelief. "Camp Tapawingo."

"That wasn't the name of ours," he said with a shake of his head. "It was called something shorter. I would have remembered a name as unusual as Tapawingo." He stared at her as if she'd had a memory lapse.

"We used to call it Camp Win for short, but it's been Camp Tapawingo from its founding day eighty years ago," Grace insisted. "I think it was named after a Cree chief." Happy memories of their shared past at the camp filled her brain. "You were so big on sports. Remember the time at camp when you got beaned by a baseball? And the next year when you broke your arm trying to catch that football?"

"Are you implying that I'm prone to breaking

bones?" Jack chuckled before he conceded, "I guess I have broken several bones over the years."

"The mark of a *real* cowboy," she teased. "Tell me where you remember the camp being located."

"Maybe three or four hours from Sunshine? It took forever to get there." His forehead pleated as he thought about it. "We went over a bunch of knolls with lots of rocks until we finally crested a hill by some farmer's field—" He stopped short when she shook her head. "What?"

"Actually, Jack, Camp Win, Tapawingo, is not quite an hour-and-a-half drive from here. And we only took the route over the hills those two times you went because roadwork diverted us." Grace smiled. "You've just demonstrated my point. We think what we remember is the truth. But we're often wrong and not only as children. Even as adults, our perceptions, our thinking get in the way of the actual truth."

"You're going to connect this to God, aren't you?" he said with a hint of resignation.

"Yes, because the only way we can really *know* God is through a personal relationship. It isn't by someone else telling us about Him. I didn't get to know you through those minimal Christmas notes you sent. I need to spend time with you, learn your thoughts and fears, talk about our lives." She checked her watch and then rose. "Goodness, it's Lizzie's bedtime. I'd better go."

"Why did you tell me all that, Grace?" Jack

looked thoughtful. "Because you think I don't remember you the way you were, that I need to get to know you again?"

"That's probably true," she agreed with a chuckle. "You do need to. But I actually said it because I believe you're operating under some misconceptions about God and I think you should find the truth about Him for yourself." She met his stare and added, "I also think you have some mistaken beliefs about me."

"Could be." The way he said it made her study him warily as he slowly stood. His expression gave nothing away. "You've helped me realize I *should* know a lot more about the woman I'm going to marry. Milt used to say power is knowledge. You better tell me more about yourself next time we talk."

"Because you need power over me?" Grace sighed wearily, wondering if she'd ever really know this man whom she'd once thought she loved. Then his inference sank in. "I *did not agree* to marry you," she enunciated clearly.

"Yet." He laughed out loud at her glower.

"Listen to me, Jack—I can't just decide to marry you because *you* want it!" Grace shook her head as if to clear it. "I'm very sorry about your loss and Lizzie's problems, truly I am. But marriage isn't a decision to be taken lightly. Added to which, I'm not at all certain that I have the ability to handle Lizzie or to be her stand-in grandmother."

"What bothers you the most?" he asked quietly.

"Everything, Jack! I'm not fifteen anymore. I'm retired now. My hair is gray!" she remonstrated.

"No, it isn't," he corrected with a funny little smile. "It's the most lovely shade of hammered silver, like a queen's crown. It suits you perfectly. But even if it was gray, so what?"

"So what?" She had no words.

"You're even more beautiful than I remembered, Gracie. And don't play the age card because you're hardly in your dotage. The nurses constantly bragged on your schedule. Sounded to me like it would make twenty-year-old women quiver." He fake-shuddered. "I know it does me."

"Don't you flatter me, Jack Prinz. It won't work now like it did all those years ago," she warned him. "I'm serious."

"So am I! I'm not some poor preacher's kid anymore, Grace. I have money so you don't have to worry about the cost of taking on Lizzie. When you marry me, everything I have will be yours," he promised. "And there's quite a lot."

"I'm not concerned about money," Grace snapped. Then she frowned. "There's no nice way to say this, but, well, I don't love you, Jack."

"That's a positive in my book. Love doesn't matter," he said quickly. Too quickly.

"Of course it matters!" She stared at him, confused, appalled and a host of other adjectives.

"Marriage is all about love. What you're proposing sounds more like a—" She scrounged for the appropriate word and came up with, "Partnership!"

"That's exactly what I want." His head sank to his chest and his voice dropped. "Sheena and I—well, it was an agreement."

"An agreement? I don't want an *agreement* marriage," she said in disgust. "It sounds like a business deal."

"It will be. Sort of. We're friends, you and I. Nothing wrong with friendship," Jack insisted.

"Not a thing," Grace backtracked, wishing she hadn't let her stupid feelings take over. "Friendship is always a blessing. But if you are intent on pursuing this idea of marriage without love— well then, it's better if we both start out with mutual understanding about exactly what you expect from me."

Did she sound disappointed that he wasn't talking about love? Grace hoped not. She didn't want Jack to know how long she'd clung to that dream, or that, truthfully, even though she'd long ago given up on it, it still hung there, in the depths of her soul, yearning.

"What I *expect*?" His expression hardened. "That's a strange thing to say. Are you hiding something, Grace?"

"Oh for land's sake—I'm not *hiding* anything, *asking* for anything, or *expecting* anything!" she said in exasperation. "But I need a clear picture of what you want from me." Somehow learning about him had become too complicated. But it was too late now to stop pressing for answers. She had to understand before she could commit to anything.

"I *want* us to get married," he said firmly.

"Yes, I got that part," she said briskly. "But I need to know a lot more than that. I need to understand your expectations for such a marriage before I can assess whether I can or want to fulfill them." She frowned at him. "And I'd prefer honesty and truth because I don't like surprises."

"You never did. I guess that hasn't changed." Suddenly Jack looked worn out and that sent a pang of regret to her heart. "Honestly?" he admitted, "I never thought that far ahead. I guess I should have."

"You're just out of the hospital. We'll talk about it more another day," she prevaricated. "And Lizzie has school tomorrow. She needs to get to bed. As do you."

"Maybe but I'm going to talk to Ben for a while. I want to hear more about their plans. I used to be a rodeo star, Gracie." Jack's chest puffed out with pride. "A good one."

"Information I was not expecting," she muttered to herself. They walked slowly back to the house and Grace called for Lizzie.

But after Jack had kissed his granddaughter good-night, after she'd helped Lizzie say her prayers and then tucked the child into bed, Grace's heart felt heavy.

An agreement? That's the kind of relationship Jack and Sheena had shared? It sounded so sad.

"Is that why I don't hear anything from You?" Grace whispered as she stared out the big picture window where sunset had faded to twilight. "Is an agreement the best I can hope for if I marry Jack?"

A laser-cut black metal plaque on the wall, lit by the lamp below, caught her attention.

"And God is able to make all grace abound toward you; that ye, always having all sufficiency in all things, may abound to every good work: 2 Corinthians 9:8."

Always having all sufficiency in all things. The words repeated in her brain.

In other words, God was in control of her life and He would ensure she had exactly what she needed. She could rest in His promise.

Grace closed her eyes and let her brain savor that security for a while, until her phone pinged. She smiled as she read Jess's text and studied the pictures of the Panama Canal.

"You made that right," she whispered as she turned out the lights. "You will with Jack, too. Won't You?"

Two days later, Jack was again enjoying hearing ideas for the rodeo, though he wasn't thrilled that Gracie still hadn't appeared at the meeting.

He felt she kept making excuses to avoid him, even though she was the one who said they should get to know each other. How were they supposed to do that if they didn't do things together?

"I'm sorry, Jack, but I have to check on Jess's house and water her garden this afternoon," she'd said yesterday. This morning it was, "I have a lunch meeting at the church about Vacation Bible School, but I'll be back for my ladies' meeting at the log house this afternoon. It might run late but I'll try to get to the rodeo meeting."

The only good thing about it was that Grace had whisked away in her own compact purple car and had thankfully shown no desire to drive his vehicle again, which now sat protected under one of the Double H's outbuildings, waiting until e could drive again. Jack felt a little wiggle of guilt about his possessiveness over that vehicle, but he quashed it. He had other issues to worry about, such as how to get Grace to marry him. So far, insisting on it hadn't worked out for him.

Grace had suggested Jack have his meals with her and Lizzie, though they had to eat outside because he couldn't climb the steps. He was glad the mornings were bright and warm. But when he'd gone there this morning for breakfast, Grace had remonstrated with him over his lack of a compliment about Lizzie's pretty hairstyle. Only then had he realized his granddaughter's great disappointment. He'd tried to make up for that, but that hadn't erased Grace's disapproval. It was Lizzie who had clued him in on a new idea to pursue Grace.

"Where did she get those flowers on the picnic table?" he'd asked while he waited with her for the bus. "They look like weeds."

"They're wildflowers. We picked them really early this morning in the meadow. Miss P. likes all flowers. Even dandelions. She said she could make a salad out of them, but if she does, I'm not eatin' it!" Lizzie's nose had wrinkled in distaste before she added, "But she likes lilacs best."

"Miss P.?" he asked, one eyebrow raised.

"I like it lots better 'n calling her Grace. 'Sides, the Calhoun kids call her that," Lizzie defended.

"Well, then, that's okay." He'd waved her goodbye and watched until the bus drove away. "Grace likes flowers, does she?" he mused as he thumped his way to a nearby bench.

Jack thought about that for a while and finally decided he'd order a big bouquet, no, several of them, so she'd be overwhelmed. Surely that would say better than any words he could come up with that he was thinking about her. He pulled out his phone and set about impressing Gracie.

Satisfied with that plan, Jack spent the next few hours watching Mandy work with her horses. She was a natural.

"You and the Double H horses belong together," he told her when she finally came over to talk.

"Thanks. They're my pride and joy. Second to Drew." The glow in her eyes as they settled on her husband said everything about their marriage. They loved each other. "Excuse me, Jack, I have to talk to Drew."

He watched them for a few minutes, surprised by the envy he felt. Would Grace ever look at him like that? He shook his head. How crazy was he? He didn't want any part of love.

"'Morning, Jack. Thought you might like a tour of the Double H." Sam glanced at his leg. "Think you can manage the passenger seat of this ATV?"

"I can try." Thanks to a fresh pain pill, Jack found the vehicle quite comfortable. As he rode, he listened to Sam's commentary. He was so interested that he was surprised when they eventually returned and stopped in front of the log house.

"Lunchtime. Ma said you and Miss P. insist on getting your own meals," he said. Jack figured something in his expression must have given away the fact that this was news to him because Sam added, "I'm guessing that cooler under the table is for you. But if you can't find anything you like, go check Ma's fridge. She's always got something to eat. See you later."

"Thanks a lot for the tour." Jack watched him drive away before thumping his way to the table on the patch of grass in front of the house. Slightly winded, he sank onto a bench and caught his breath. A note was stuck to the top of the cooler.

Jack: Cheese sandwich and iced tea inside for your lunch. I know you don't want to bother Bonnie.

Yes, he did, especially since he was sure that lady would offer a lot more than a plain old cheese sandwich to eat. But then, he was a guest, an un-invited one, and he didn't want to be a nuisance.

The note was signed, *Have a nice day. Grace.*

Nice? Jake shrugged, opened the cooler and unwrapped the sandwich with disgust. If he could drive, he'd head into town and get something good to eat. Hey, maybe he could catch a ride!

He closed the cooler and grabbed his crutches, but then remembered Grace's kind generosity to him and Lizzie. She'd taken over his granddaughter's care without complaining, even canceled her trip of a lifetime for them. It would undoubtedly hurt her feelings if he didn't eat what she'd left.

If he wanted her to marry him, he'd better not blow this.

Reluctantly, Jack sat down and ate his meager sandwich plus an apple he'd tucked in his pocket after breakfast. Then he lifted a bottle of iced tea away from the ice pack in the cooler. As he sipped it, he surveyed the ranch and thought about Grace. Like her, these folks were really nice people who unstintingly reached out to anyone in need.

That's when Jack suddenly knew that nothing

about his former plans, or even his latest floral brainwave, was going to work.

Grace Partridge, the strong, determined woman she was now, would not be persuaded to marry him because of some flamboyant bouquets. The Gracie he'd known had never put much stock in ostentatious gestures and he doubted that had changed. She *was* a woman who demanded quality, like her car. It was a compact, yes, but he recognized that it was top of the line of a prestigious brand, and the newest model. And hadn't he overheard someone at the hospital say Grace had paid for her friend to take *her* trip? So his money would hardly impress her, which he'd known but hadn't wanted to admit.

Therefore, if the lady wanted flowers, Jack was pretty sure she could buy them for herself. In fact, she had! He recalled the bundle of blooms she'd brought home from the hospital. They must be starting to wilt by now, but they still sat in a vase in the big picture window. Because Gracie was about way more than pretty flowers.

What had she said? She was waiting for some heavenly confirmation about marrying him?

Jack didn't know about heaven, but he figured *he* was going to have to show her he was worthy of that honor. But how?

Miss P. likes all flowers. Even dandelions. Lizzie's earlier comment echoed in his head.

Dandelions? Jack glanced at the cast on his leg.

A clock chimed the half hour. Twelve thirty. Grace would be back soon for her ladies' meeting. If Jack was going to do anything, it had to be now.

Some laugh at me. I'm the silly old spinster librarian. The memory of her face, embarrassed, pained, but most of all wounded by that admission, cut to his heart. If there was one thing Jack couldn't abide it was someone's suffering because of a thoughtless comment. He'd been the target of those too many times to count.

"Nobody's going to laugh today, Gracie," he muttered. "Except maybe you. At me."

With a grunt of silent determination, Jack rose awkwardly and made his way across the yard. Sam had shown him all the special places on the ranch. They'd even stopped to overlook a beautiful grassy area the family cherished. Sam had called it Peace Meadow and now Jack recalled seeing a burst of bright yellow right next to a picnic table.

It took more than twenty minutes to negotiate the uneven terrain to the meadow, fifteen more to contort his body to bend enough so he could reach the yellow blooms. Then he realized he had no way to hold the flowers *and* manipulate his crutches, so he tucked the stems into his shirt pocket and began the grueling trip back to the log house with his casted leg throbbing.

Several of the ranch hands passed, staring at him in disbelief, then half-hidden smirks. Jack felt all kinds of a fool but he pressed on. By the time he reached the picnic table, his watch read one thirty. Grace would be here any minute.

Jack grabbed his iced-tea bottle, filled it from the outside tap and thrust the dandelions stems into it. Somehow, he managed to hold it under his arm. Then, summoning his last bit of energy, Jack worked his way back to the table and triumphantly placed the flower-filled glass on the center of the picnic table.

Desperate for relief from his aching leg, he forced through the pain to walk to the main house where he headed for his room, thrilled that it was on the first floor. Once there he collapsed on the bed and closed his eyes, willing the agony to recede.

If that didn't prove to Gracie that he was good husband material—with a sigh of pure weariness, Jack let his mind sink into oblivion.

Chapter Five

"Oh, my word!"

Later that afternoon, for the first time in living memory, Grace fell speechless. All she could do was stand back and watch.

Her entire ladies' group gawked, too, while delivery people filed through the door, each one bearing a massive arrangement. First came roses—the deep yellow, long-stemmed ones Grace had always adored. *Texas roses?* Of course, the sender had to be Jack.

Then came lilies, enormous Asiatic ones in unbelievable hues of persimmon, lime green and aqua. Following them, perky gerbera daisies in a rainbow of primary colors that held the eye and filled the room with joy. Their bright tones were a perfect foil for a delicate orchid, white and trembling in its massive pot. Last, a gigantic flowering hydrangea was placed by the side of the kitchen island because there simply was nowhere else.

"That last one matches your eyes perfectly, Grace," Lyn Chance, their club president, enthused. "A perfect cross between blue and violet."

"Who are they from?" Val Harper wondered.

Grace ignored their curiosity and offered a tip, but apparently, that had already been taken care of because the flower bearers declined before hurrying away. Silence stretched across the room while everyone's gaze moved from one floral display to the next.

Cheeks burning, Grace eased the hydrangea plant out of the way so she could sit, fully aware that the overwhelming aroma in the crowded space, not to mention the ladies' curiosity, was going to make it difficult to concentrate on the purpose of this meeting.

"You're probably wondering why I called this meeting," she began.

"They're from that man, aren't they?" Carol Cormel nodded. "The grandfather of the girl you're caring for."

"I believe so, yes," Grace agreed. *Jack, you are so going to get such an earful...* She swallowed her irritation and lifted her chin. "I'm sorry for the interruption. Now, I was explaining about the rodeo the folks here on the Double H hope to sponsor. I thought perhaps our ladies' group could contribute."

"We don't even know if it's a go yet," Martha Brown objected. "And why don't we take a minute to admire your gorgeous blooms? Aren't you taking pictures to show Jess what your admirer sent?"

"He's not my admirer," Grace sputtered.

"What is he then?" Patt Parker glanced around, obviously expecting the others to offer their opinions.

"He's an old boyfriend," Lenora Peters said with a wink. "From back in the day." She flicked the ends of her newly bleached blond strands off her shoulders with an authoritative nod.

"Hardly a boyfriend, Lenora, though, yes, I knew Jack in school," Grace informed her coolly. "When I was *fifteen*," she emphasized. "I haven't seen or spoken to him since."

"Well, he sure seems to know you because these *are* your favorite flowers." President Lyn glanced at the others meaningfully.

"Perhaps Jack asked Mina at the flower store what Grace preferred," Gail Trask suggested.

"Or maybe one of the nurses told him." That was Carol again. She volunteered at the hospital and would almost certainly ask the staff for more information about Jack next time she went in.

That thought caused tension. Grace hated being the source of all this speculation. Every one of them would spread the news all over town that someone had sent Grace a mass of flowers. Gossip would be rampant.

She swallowed her frustration and glanced at her watch.

"Ladies, I don't want to be rude, but Lizzie will soon be home from school…" She let it trail away, hoping they'd get the hint.

"Yes, and I have several errands to run before I have to start dinner, so we'd best conclude this meeting." Lyn called them back to order. "Grace, you're living here on the Double H so it should be easy for you to ask the Calhouns more about this rodeo. Perhaps you can get an idea as to a possible date, how many contestants they would accept, that kind of thing."

"Me? But—" Grace swallowed hard. Arguing would only draw more attention. She nodded, accepting the assignment.

"Carol, you and Patt draw up a menu we could serve and price out how much supplies will cost us. Simple things like burgers, hot dogs, chili. Nothing complicated," their president insisted. "I'll check into permits and such."

"What should Lenora and I do?" Martha asked, glancing at her nearby friends.

"I'm thinking we'll need prizes so we can hold some kind of raffle. See what ideas you can come up with," Lyn ordered. "Now, are we all agreed Sunshine Ladies' Group will assist the Double H rodeo to fund-raise for repairs to Camp Tapawingo?" She noted the raised hands and smiled. "Unanimous. Perfect. Anything else?"

The women had many more ideas and each was noted. Lyn was ready to adjourn, but Grace had something else on her mind.

"I think we should invite Drew's wife, Mandy, to join our group," she suggested. "Not only because she's the one who teaches the kids around here how to ride, or because she's won so many rodeo trophies in the past. But more because we need new members in our group and I think she'd be a great addition."

"Good idea. Perhaps we could ask the other two Calhoun wives, as well. Everyone agree Grace should ask them? Good," Lyn said when the others nodded.

Grace wanted to object but the school bus was pulling into the yard.

"Motion for adjournment is carried. Thank you, girls. I think we're going to have a wonderful rodeo fund-raiser. Thanks to Grace for hosting us."

Grace nodded absently, noting the women's curious looks as the Calhoun children left the bus. Lizzie was last. If only they'd left *before* she'd returned. Speculation in town about Jack and Lizzie was rife, aided, no doubt, by the child's too-small and, though Grace had tried to repair it, tattered clothing. That was another item on her growing to-do list.

Each woman waited to be introduced. Some prodded poor Lizzie about her age, her former residence and especially about her grandfather. When someone wondered what had happened to Lizzie's grandmother, Grace drew the line.

"I'm sorry, but we have an appointment," she

said, smiling as nicely as she was able. "Thank you all for coming."

"They must be going to see her Jack."

Her Jack? Grace pursed her lips.

"Probably to thank him for those flowers, which must have cost him a bundle."

"Is he rich?"

Grace closed the door on the whispers carried by the spring breeze.

"They sure ask a lot of questions," Lizzie grumbled. Her eyes widened when she saw all the flowers. "Wow!" She grinned. "They're from Pops, aren't they?"

"I think so, yes, though I haven't seen a card." Grace poured a glass of milk and set out three cookies left over from the meeting. "Here you go." She made herself a very strong mug of instant coffee. "Have your snack, dear. Then we're going to see your pops."

"I wanna talk to him, too." Lizzie sat down at the table. "I gotta get some new clothes. My jeans tore some more today. Pops said he was gonna get me new ones a'fore, but I guess he forgot."

"No doubt your grandfather has been very busy," Grace grumbled caustically, glaring at the flowers. He might as well have hired a billboard. Florist Mina Baker would gladly tell anyone who asked everything she knew. Actually, Mina would probably tell them even if they didn't ask.

"Where'd you get the dandelions?" Lizzie

asked as cookie crumbs fell from her lips. "You're not making salad out of 'em, are you?" Her expression grew sulky.

"What dandelions?" Grace followed Lizzie to the window, saw the flowers sitting on the picnic table. "I didn't pick those. You didn't either?" Puzzled when Lizzie shook her head, Grace went outside and opened the cooler. The plastic wrap from the sandwich was neatly folded atop the ice block. Her gaze lifted to the table. The dandelion vase was the empty bottle from the iced tea she'd left with the sandwich.

Jack picked dandelions? For me? Then why send a ton of flowers?

She returned inside to sip her coffee while Lizzie chatted on about her day. Grace's empathy for the child rose when she asked about Jack for the third time. The poor girl seemed to constantly worry about her grandfather's absence.

"I'm sure he's fine, dear. I believe his meeting will soon be over." She'd chafed at missing it, but it was too late now. She'd already seen a few cars leaving the yard by the main house. "We'll go find him in a few minutes."

"Okay. Why were those ladies here?" Lizzie asked next.

"We're going to help with a rodeo they're planning to have here at the ranch," Grace explained.

"You should ask Pops to help. He and my dad had lots of rodeos at our ranch. I won a ribbon once." Lizzie's voice dropped at the memory. Her face grew gloomier as she finished her milk.

"I think Jack's already offered to help, dear." Hoping to chase away the blues, Grace continued. "The money that's raised will go toward fixing up a kids' camp."

"What's this camp like?" Lizzie wanted to know.

"It's great. There's a lake to swim in and boating and story time and wiener roasts with s'mores. Lots of fun things." She watched the girl's eyes brighten and decided to take a chance. "I'm sure many of your school chums will go this summer. Would you like to go, too?"

Lizzie suddenly went silent. Her tiger eyes darkened as they narrowed. "No," she said firmly.

"Maybe you would want to if you knew more about it," Grace said nonchalantly. "I'll tell you some more about it later and maybe you'll change your mind."

"Is it just for kids?" Lizzie asked. Grace nodded. She shook her head. "Then I don't wanna go. I don't wanna leave Pops."

Grace was going to object but thought better of it. Maybe with time, after Lizzie had settled in and when the other kids talked up camp, she would change her mind. Best not to press her right now.

"If you're all finished, you can put those dishes

in the dishwasher and wash up. Then we'll go find—"

Something hitting the door interrupted her. She opened it and looked outside. Jack stood by the table, tossing pebbles back and forth from one hand to the other.

"Hey there, Gracie," he said with a smile. "You missed the rodeo meeting."

"Yes, I know." She refused to explain.

He peered past her. His smile suddenly transformed into startled, and somewhat guilty surprise. "Oh."

"Oh, indeed." Grace raised her eyebrows and waited for an explanation.

"Hi, Pops." Lizzie raced down the steps and threw her arms around his waist. "Nice flowers. Hey, we gotta go get me some clothes. My jeans tore again. It was 'barrassing.'"

"I forgot we were going to do that." He hugged her, then asked, "Gracie, can we buy kids' clothes in Sunshine?"

So, he wasn't going to discuss the fact that he'd turned the log cabin into a greenhouse? Very well, neither would she.

"That was on my to-do list to talk to you about. I believe we can, though I've never actually bought children's clothes." She picked up her purse. "I assume so since the town has lots of children. If we're going to shop, we'd better hurry. It's already well past four o'clock."

"We're going in your car?" he asked, his voice unusually hesitant.

"Unless you'd rather I drive yours?" Grace hoped he'd decline. She didn't like trying to manipulate that big vehicle.

"Yours is fine. Great, in fact." The response came quickly, perhaps a little too quickly.

Grace paused in helping Lizzie fasten her seat belt to study him, but Jack was easing into her car and she couldn't tell if he was being sincere so she shrugged and got into the driver's seat.

During their trip into Sunshine, she explained more about the camp where, as a child, she had spent so many happy times.

"Did you go fishing?" Lizzie sounded anxious.

"That's where I learned to fish," Grace said with a smile. "The lake is amazing. Your grandfather—" She stopped, irritated that somehow she'd let Jack into the conversation.

"Pops loves fishing, don'tcha, Pops? Me 'n him usta fish all the time at our ranch. But after my mom and dad died, he had ta sell it." Lizzie fell silent for a few minutes before blurting, "I can't go to camp. I gotta be here in case Pops dies. But I don't want Pops to die."

I don't either.

Grace's irritation evaporated. It was the truth. Why pretend otherwise? Jack's brashness, self-confidence and need to push boundaries had always been his strongest features. No point in expecting that his basic personality would have changed, so what was the point of being angry about some beautiful flowers?

"I'm not dying anytime soon, Sweet Pea," Jack assured Lizzie.

"But you might. You're old, Pops."

Grace smothered a laugh when he asserted, "Not that old!" in a disgruntled tone.

"Tell you what, Lizzie," Grace offered, tongue in cheek. "We'll pray for your pops. God can do many wonderful things, even for old people."

"Like make Pops not be too old to play soccer?" Lizzie waited a few moments then sighed. "I didn't think so."

"I didn't say God couldn't do that, dear. But Pops does have a broken leg." Grace steered into a parking spot in front of general store, feeling totally out of her depth. It was so hard to know the right thing to say, comforting but not unrealistic. "Sometimes we have to wait for God to answer." *Take your own advice*, her brain scolded.

"'Kay." Lizzie got out of the car, bouncing from one foot to the other as she waited for Jack to exit the vehicle. "I like going to school okay," she announced when he was finally standing and able to hold her hand. "But I'd rather be with Pops."

"I'm sure." Grace shared a smile with Jack. "But sometimes we have to do things we'd rather not."

"Why?" Lizzie demanded.

Out of answers, Grace glanced meaningfully at Jack. And he got the message.

"We'd better think about clothes shopping now and stop asking so many questions." He urged Lizzie inside the store.

When they reached the children's clothing, she released his hand and went to see what was offered. Grace tried to note which colors the little girl gravitated to.

"Kids' questions are the hardest, aren't they?" Jack murmured from behind her. "I'm never sure if I'm answering hers or just providing fodder for the next ones."

"I know the feeling." Grace summoned her courage. "Thank you for the flowers, Jack. They're beautiful."

"Which ones?" he asked, surprising her.

"Well of course I like them all." Grace tried to appear cool and collected, though her heart did that stupid racing thing it always did when this man stood too close to her. "Where did you find the dandelions?"

"Clearly, the dandelions win the flower contest." Jack barked out a laugh, his face wreathed in a smile. "I found them in Peace Meadow."

"The meadow?" She gaped at him. "But—how did you get there?"

"Walked. Or limped. Or hopped. Whatever." He grimaced. "I'm sorry if I embarrassed you at your ladies' meeting with the other ones. They were an impulse decision. Then I decided to get the dandelions because Lizzie said you liked them best, but I forgot to cancel the florist's order." Jack's woebegone expression made her chuckle.

"Good thing you didn't. Mina would have told the entire town you'd backed out and she'd lost a big sale. The gossip would be never ending."

"You care about the town gossiping about you, don't you, Gracie?" he asked with a smile that suddenly looked strangled. Grace turned to see why. Lizzie stood holding three frilly organza dresses. "You want *those* for school, Sweet Pea?" he asked with a gulp.

Grace knew that if his granddaughter said yes, he'd buy them, so she cleared her throat ready to insert her opinion. But there was no need. Lizzie was a very smart girl.

"'Course not, Pops," she said with an eye roll. "These are fancy dresses. I just like 'em."

"They're very nice," Grace agreed. "That pink one would be lovely with your hair and eyes. How about if we set it aside and choose some school clothes? Want to start with tops?" Lizzie nodded. "How about these?"

For an almost six-year-old, Lizzie was very definite in what she wanted.

"This blue one is nice. And I like the flowers on the green one. Not gray. But I like this yellow one. What are these flowers called, Pops?"

"Plain old daisies." He nodded his agreement to Grace about the garments she held.

"Three more tops and two sweaters," Grace said. "Then we'll move on to jeans."

"'Kay." Lizzie found the tops and added two T-shirts. "'Cause the Calhoun kids have them," she said before moving on to jeans and then shorts.

Grace left them trying on sneakers while she scooped up some new underwear and socks for the child, to replace the shabby ones she'd laundered last night. When she returned from paying for them, Lizzie and Jack were discussing sandals.

"I don't like them. Sand and dirt get in my toes," she argued, her chin jutting out stubbornly.

"If you want to wear those nice summer dresses you like, you should wear sandals, not sneakers," Jack contended just as stubbornly. When Lizzie glared at him, Jack turned to Grace. "Tell her," he insisted.

"You're not really going to be in sand and dirt when you wear the dress and sandals, Lizzie," she offered placatingly. "We should get the pink dress."

"Why?" Lizzie tipped her head to one side.

"For Easter Sunday next week. Everyone in Sunshine dresses up for Easter," she explained. "Clothes like that dress and those sandals are for church and special occasions."

"Oh. Special times." Lizzie's face brightened. "Like when you an' Pops get married?"

Grace blinked and began backpedaling.

"I'm not sure if or when that might happen," she said carefully. "But for a wedding…" *My wedding?* The very idea made her heart race. "I think that if there was to be a wedding, we'd get an even more special dress for you. This is a Sunday dress. We could get two, but we also need some more casual Sunday clothes." She was slightly amused that after having restocked her own entire wardrobe for the past several months to shed her dowdy image, she was now repeating the exercise with Lizzie. "Do you like these?" She held up three cotton outfits.

Lizzie nodded eagerly.

"This is a lot of clothes," Jack grumbled, trying to manage the stack as he leaned on one crutch. "Are you sure we need so much?"

"Not if you have other clothing for Lizzie hidden somewhere," she said, pulling over a cart and setting everything in it.

"We don't." Lizzie hugged a sigh. "I got too big for everything. Pops couldn't even get my old T-shirts over my head 'cause it grew so fat!"

"Not fat, Lizzie," Jack protested but she ignored his interruption.

"Anyhow, Pops said there was no point in trying to squeeze me into them or packing them when I couldn't wear them anymore, so we gave them away." Her face saddened. "'Cept for the sweater Mama made me. But it doesn't fit neither."

"Either," Grace corrected automatically. She'd seen that sweater last night and it certainly didn't fit, although maybe—

"Can I get a jacket, too, Pops?" Lizzie stared up at her Pops beseechingly. "I might need one if it rains. It wouldn't cost too much, would it?"

"Sweet Pea, nothing you want will cost too much, so don't you worry about that," Jack assured her.

The tenderness on this grandfather's face and the gentle way he slid his hand lovingly over Lizzie's head told Grace everything about Jack's love for this child. The lines around his mouth also told her he was hurting.

"Dear, why don't you go look at the jackets while your grandpa and I sit on these chairs?" When Lizzie frowned, she bent near and whispered, "I think Pops's leg is hurting him."

"Okay. Can I get polka dots?" she whispered back with a cheeky grin.

"You bring your favorites and we'll decide together." Grace savored the little girl's excitement as she skipped to the rack and deliberated over a red-and-white polka-dot rain jacket. "That's her favorite," she told Jack quietly.

"It doesn't look like it's very good quality," he said with a frown.

"It doesn't really matter because it will only

last her this year. Then she'll have a growth spurt and need a new one next season," Grace reasoned. "Besides, it's a good time for her to start learning about the value of things. If it tatters and tears, then you can explain about quality."

"Lizzie's a bit young for that, surely?" Jack said with some incredulity.

"You'd be surprised. She's smart and she picks things up very quickly." Grace hid her amusement when he focused on his granddaughter intently, as if searching for some physical sign of her mental aptitude.

"I want to get her a pair of boots, too," he said firmly.

"She's already chosen some. They're at the bottom of the basket. If it rains as it's supposed to tonight, she'll need them." Grace checked the weather forecast on her phone. "One-hundred-percent chance," she said.

"Not *those* boots. Riding boots. I gave away her old ones. Like everything else, they were too small." Jack was staring at something. Grace turned to see what it was. Riding gear.

"I thought you told me Lizzie has refused to ride since her parents' deaths?" She stared at him, waiting for the truth.

"She did, but once she sees those new red boots, she'll give in and get up on a pony sure as shootin'," he argued with a grin. "She loved her old ones. They were white."

"Talk about impractical," she mumbled, then cleared her throat. "Jack, I really think you need to wait on that. Give her time—"

"She's had enough time," he insisted. "Besides, the Prinz family are ranchers, and ranchers ride."

"You're not a rancher anymore, Jack," she reminded, but he ignored her and called to Lizzie. "Come, see what I found."

Lizzie obediently came, lugging her two rain jacket selections. Her face glowed, her eyes shone with pleasure. "Aren't they pretty, Pops?"

"They're both lovely, dear," Grace interjected before Jack could speak. Maybe if he had time to think about this, he'd change his mind. "Which do *you* prefer?"

"I like the red one best, but if I get the blue one, the boots will match it," she said thoughtfully.

"Do you want them to match?" Grace asked in surprise.

"Uh-huh. 'Cause when *you* wear stuff, it matches. Like your belt and your purse match. An' your sweater has the same color in it as your pants." Lizzie smiled. "You always look really pretty, Miss P."

"Why, thank you, dear." Taken off guard by the compliment, Grace wasn't sure what to say.

But she wished she'd said something when Jack declared, "We're going to get you some new riding boots, Sweet Pea."

And Lizzie said, "No."

* * *

Jack could feel Gracie's glacial glare. He also saw Lizzie's set face and the glint of rebellion in her dark eyes. But this was important, so he pushed.

"Sweet Pea, you have to get riding again. You know you love it," he wheedled when her chin thrust out. "But your old boots are too small and we gave them away, remember?"

"I don't want new boots, Pops. I told you. I'm not going to ride anymore. Ever," she added, as if she thought he would argue with her. "An' if that means I can't have the new clothes, I don't care." She turned her back on him and walked to the front of the store.

"Lizzie!" He blinked and glanced at Grace for an explanation. Bad idea.

"Why did you do that, Jack?" The almost-black shade of her eyes and the tight pinch of her lips said Grace was furious. "Why did you have to spoil a perfectly lovely time? She was smiling and enjoying herself picking out new things. Why couldn't you let that be? Why must you force everyone to your will?"

"But—" He frowned. "She has to ride again. Someday."

"Why? Because it's what *you* want?" Grace's scathing tone and scornful glare hurt more than he'd expected.

Jack wanted her to think well of him, to prove

he wasn't as bad at parenting as he'd said. But it was obvious he was because he kept messing up and proving it.

"There is a reason Lizzie is refusing to ride, Jack. Why don't you try to find out what that reason is, *without* browbeating her?"

"But—"

"You said you weren't a good father to Cade," she reminded him softly. "Well, here's your chance to make up for that. Be a good parent to Lizzie by letting her figure out who she is. She isn't your son, Jack. She's her own person and she's lost everything that made up her world. Her parents, her home, her friends. All she has left is you."

"I know, but—" Again she interrupted him, this time with a shake of her head.

"Nobody wants to feel they've been pushed into something. She isn't going to be forced onto a horse and suddenly realize she loves it. Trying to press the issue will only alienate her." She studied him with a calculating gaze that seemed to peer into his very soul.

Jack was miffed that Gracie, who was neither a parent nor a grandparent, would lecture *him*. And yet, the truth was that he hadn't been able to help Lizzie so far. Wasn't that exactly why he'd come to Sunshine?

"Well, then what *am* I supposed to do?" he challenged.

"Love her, Jack. Be there when she needs you. And give her some time to find her own way."

Gracie walked away then, leaving him to push a cart full of little girls' stuff while nursing a full head of steam. Then he saw Lizzie standing at the front of the store, shoulders hunched defensively, looking forlorn and miserable, and his irritation melted while his gut twisted.

"Blasted females," Jack muttered in disgust. He shoved his crutches in the cart, grabbed the handle, and slowly made his way to the cash register. "Ring it up," he ordered the woman standing there. "Please."

"I don't need them, Pops." Lizzie's whisper came from the area of his right hip. He hadn't even noticed her come over. "I can keep wearing these ones."

"No, you can't, Sweet Pea," he assured her, striving for joviality. "Your knee is busting out of those jeans." He lifted his head and met Grace's scrutiny. "She'd have my head if I let you go to school for one more day in those old things." He let his hand graze across Lizzie's dark hair while a tsunami of affection swelled inside. "Grace is a very fashionable lady, Sweet Pea. We don't want to embarrass her, especially if she's going to marry us."

"Jack! I never said—"

"Add in that stuff she's carrying, too, will you?" he butted in to tell the salesclerk, inclining his head toward Gracie, who held several balls of white wool. "Might as well put it all on one tab." He handed over his credit card.

"I'll pay you later," Grace murmured.

"Don't bother. I'm sure you'll do something wonderful with it that everyone will love," Jack said caustically, then felt like he'd been doused with ice cubes when he noticed her grave expression matched Lizzie's.

Why was it he could never get it right? Why was he always making mistakes with the very people who mattered most to him?

Chapter Six

"Does it look nice?" Lizzie asked, twirling in her new dress.

"It's perfect for Easter Sunday. And here's a little sunhat I crocheted to go with it." Grace set the tiny lace confection on her head and smiled. "You look beautiful, dear."

"Why do I need to wear a hat?" Lizzie asked, staring at herself in the mirror.

"You don't *have* to. It's just a tradition we have at our church. My mom used to call them Easter bonnets," she explained, fixing her own feathered affair to the top of her head.

"That sounds old-fashioned." Lizzie's nose wrinkled. "Do we look old-fashioned?"

Gravel rasped against the door.

"That's your pops. Why don't you go ask him how you look?" Grace suggested, feeling a bit smug with herself. She'd chosen this particular dress because it made her feel beautiful. Would Jack think so, too?

"Pops, do I look old-fashioned with this hat?" Lizzie asked through the open door. Their disagreement at the store had been settled the same evening when Jack had apologized to his granddaughter, who had instantly forgiven him, and the subject of her riding had been shelved.

Grace had accepted his apology without comment.

"Old-fashioned?" He shook his head. "Not hardly, Sweet Pea." He shook his head at her, his grin wide and loving. "You look so pretty."

Grace moved into the open doorway, keeping her expression blank as his gaze slid to her. The darkening gold eyes widened.

"You both look very, uh, pretty." His voice emerged like a low growl.

"Oh." Taken off guard by his penetrating scrutiny, Grace scrambled to find an innocuous comment. "Thank you. I, um——"

"Pops," Lizzie said in her scolding voice. "Miss P. an' me look a lot better than *pretty*." She shot a quick grin at Grace. "Are all those ladies gonna be at church, the ones who saw your flowers?" She pantomimed someone fawning priggishly. "The Googly Eyes, I call them."

"I think so, Lizzie. If you want to know the truth, I was a little *googly-eyed* myself when all those flowers arrived." Grace lifted one eyebrow and fixed her focus on Jack. "That delivery seemed a bit over-the-top, even for you."

"Nothing's over-the-top for my future wife." His eyes sparkled. In fact, his whole demeanor seemed somehow lighter, more cheerful. She hated to douse his pleasure, but she wouldn't allow him to keep up with his incorrect assumptions.

"I haven't agreed to marry you."

"Not yet." Jack shrugged as if it was a foregone conclusion. "But you will. You won't be able to help yourself."

"You should work on that lack of self-esteem," Grace grumbled while trying to suppress the flutter of irritation inside. "Meanwhile, I don't think arrogance is helping your case."

"I'm sorry. I was just teasing you." Jack *did* look sorry, for now.

Only, she'd never felt certain he was sincere in his apologies, and that lay at the root of her hesitation to really consider his proposal. That, the lack of love between them or an affirmation from God.

"Did you like the flowers?" he asked now.

"They were lovely. Huge blooms. They're not quite as spectacular now, but I have some pictures I sent to Jess." Grace found the photos on her phone and gave it to him. She wished she hadn't when he viewed them and came upon others which he peered at with intensity. Annoyed and feeling he'd invaded her privacy, she took her phone from him and tucked it into her bag. "Thank you for sending them."

"You're welcome." He was silent for a moment, his brow furrowing as he studied her. Then his focus slipped to Lizzie. "How is school going, Sweet Pea? I forgot to ask you."

"It's—" Lizzie stopped when Grace cleared her throat. "Fine," she substituted after a short pause. "I already know the book they're learning, but that's okay 'cause Miss P. and me got some new ones from the library and they're really cool."

Grace loved the way Lizzie lit up at the delight of a new book. The girl reminded her of herself at that age, learning to read and then devouring everything.

"That was nice of her." Jack smiled at Grace. "Wasn't it?"

"Yep." Lizzie tipped her head to the side. "Do you know 'bout Laura Ingalls Wilder, Pops?"

"Boy, do I." He mussed her hair and chuckled. "Your dad loved those books, too. When you were still a wee baby, I think he read every one of them to you about three times."

"Really?" Lizzie looked stunned by his comment. "Then Dad an' me liked the same things?"

"That's for sure. You could almost have been twins. You liked to ride. He liked to ride. Your favorite riding pants were black. So were his. You had a gray Stetson and so did he. You were like two peas in a pod." Grace cleared her throat meaningfully, but Jack ignored her. "Do you like living on a ranch again, Sweet Pea? Seeing all those lovely horses galloping in the paddocks."

"The Calhoun kids feed them sometimes, but

I don't go with them." Lizzie crossed her arms over her chest and stared at the animals.

"Oh. That's too bad," Jack said, but in a relaxed way, as if in passing. "You used to like our horses a lot. You and your dad would feed them carrots, remember?" When Lizzie didn't respond, he asked, "So what do you want to do for fun?"

Grace sat on a bench beside the picnic table to listen. Though she pretended disinterest in their conversation, she would jump in the moment he pushed Lizzie. When he didn't, her thoughts strayed to the subject that seemed to dog her lately.

Why hadn't God shown her the next step? Was it because He was putting her out to pasture? Wasn't she good for anything anymore?

Naturally, she liked Lizzie and would do her best for the girl. But that didn't mean she was going to marry Jack. No doubt it would take some explaining to get him to understand that, but she'd do it when Lizzie wasn't listening in. Automatically, Grace began to pray about it. It was only when the lack of talking penetrated her consciousness that she opened her eyes.

"We'd better get going to church, Lizzie," Grace said after she'd checked her watch. Jack was staring at her. It seemed only polite to ask, "Are you coming to the Easter service with us?"

He and Lizzie started laughing.

"Does that mean yes?" she asked quizzically.

When they continued to laugh, she frowned. "What's so funny?"

"Pops said he wondered if you'd sleep until he changed his clothes for church," Lizzie informed her. "He thinks I wear you out. Do I do that, Miss P.?"

"Not at all," she denied, ignoring Jack's smirk at her half-truth. "We get along fine. You're a very nice person to share the cabin with. I don't know if I was a good roommate at first. I've lived by myself for a long time. But I'm getting used to having someone there all the time." She checked her watch again. "We'll have to leave soon. How long will you need to change?"

"Five minutes to get to the house and five to change," Jack promised.

"I could drive you over?" she offered.

"It will take me too long to get in and out of the car," he said as he settled his crutches in place. "But you could pick me up there."

"Good idea." She watched him leave. "I wonder if I should ask the Calhoun brothers to install a ramp for him," she mused aloud.

"Pops won't like that," Lizzie said, shaking her head.

"How do you know that, dear?" Grace grabbed her car keys and led the way outside.

"'Cause he said so. Sorta." Lizzie's face squished up in thought. "He said he don't want no dumb lady friend of yours to say he's too—

um, old," she said after a slight pause, "to marry you." She climbed in the car and fastened her belt. "Pops used different words but I'm not s'posed to say 'em."

"I get the general thought. Thank you, Lizzie." Grace almost laughed out loud as she drove across the yard to pick up Jack.

She'd been uneasy at the thought of Jack attending the service with them. But knowing that he was having doubts about their relationship, as she was, somehow made her feel better when the big man squeezed into her little car a few minutes later.

"C'n we have pizza after church?" Lizzie panned a beseeching expression in the rearview mirror. "I love pizza."

"She does," Jack agreed.

"Well." Grace considered it. "I don't know if we have the ingredients, though I guess we could shop for them before we go home."

"Why don't we go out for lunch?" Jack asked. "You've been doing a lot of cooking for us since I got out of the hospital. How about if I treat you and Sweet Pea to an Easter brunch at that new place just outside of town?"

Grace studied him in surprise—surprise because the idea appealed immensely. She *was* weary. Lizzie was a dear child, but she wasn't used to the constant attention a child required.

"Can we, Miss P.?"

"Why not? I've never been there so it will be new for all of us. And you don't have to buy, Jack." Grace tried to shrug off her hurt feelings. "I was only a librarian, but I am not in need of money."

"I wasn't meaning you were, Gracie. It's just that—I've already dumped a lot on you, is all," Jack insisted.

"Very well then. Thank you. I accept your invitation." Ashamed she hadn't been more gracious, she drove into the church lot, fully aware of the interested gazes that followed their halting progress into the church.

Let them stare, Grace decided as she proudly lifted her chin. This was a place of worship. They had come to hear what God wanted to say to them. She sure hoped He would enlighten her with some nugget of inspiration that would tell her what to do about Jack.

This was *not* his father's church.

Sitting next to Gracie, Jack noted a remarkable difference. The music for one thing. Bright, happy songs that lifted you up. Everyone singing lustily, not the weak, half-hearted drone he remembered. The decor here was inspiring, too. Shades of purple, intense and dark that reminded him of Grace, and then increasingly lighter tones, drawing your eye upward, above the pulpit to a rough-hewn empty cross. Since it was Easter, pure white lilies sat everywhere, their heady fragrance filling the sanctuary. They were interspersed with buckets of daffodils and tulips that added a fresh spring ambiance.

But it was the people who impressed Jack the most. Not, he supposed, that they were much different from others. Except this congregation smiled and shook his hand, welcoming him as if they wanted him to feel he belonged among them. Had he ever felt he belonged in any of his father's churches?

"It's nice here, isn't it, Pops?" Lizzie whispered as she cuddled her hand into his when they sat after singing a hymn he vaguely remembered as his mother's favorite. "Everyone looks happy."

He nodded before once more turning his attention toward the front. A man in a wheelchair was pushed there and handed a microphone. The pianist played a quiet introduction. And then the man began to sing.

Jack stared in shock as an amazing lyrical tenor voice emerged from that frail body. The melodic words told of coming to a garden alone and then walking and talking with God in a personal way that Jack had never managed to achieve. The music compelled him to close his eyes and imagine such close commune with his creator. A sense of holy awe held him in its grip as the notes wove around him. When the last sound faded to silence, he was left with a wistful sadness that he might never again achieve such a divine connection. And he wanted to.

Jack couldn't suppress a regretful sigh as the man was wheeled away. The piano's last notes faded, but the vivid picture the singer had painted remained. Was that what a true relationship with God was like? Why did it seem so important to build that rapport?

He startled when Grace's hand rested on his arm for a moment. Her gaze held his, her eyes shining, as if she was ready to shed tears. She'd felt it, too?

"He is risen," Pastor Ed said as he stepped behind the pulpit.

"He is risen indeed," the congregation responded in unison.

"Who was the man who came as a baby, preached a new way to God, died and then rose again?" Using a timeline, he drew a clear vision of God's purpose in sending His son to provide a way for all men to come to Him.

As he listened, Jack was reminded of the many times he'd sat through sermons. Had the meaning of Easter ever been explained so clearly? Or was it simply that he'd been too deaf to hear?

All he knew was that it was over too quickly and he was left with a gnawing hunger to learn more.

"Did you enjoy our Easter service?" Grace asked as they waited to exit their pew.

"Very much," he told her.

"You sound surprised." Her purple-blue eyes twinkled. "As if you didn't expect to."

"I didn't."

"I'd be interested to hear why." She didn't wait for his answer but took advantage of a sudden opening to step into the aisle, leaving space for him to swing his crutches free. "Come, Lizzie," she said. "You'll have to finish coloring your picture later."

Once in the foyer, Gracie introduced Jack to a number of people, including the pastor.

"I'd love to get together sometime, Jack," Pastor Ed offered. "I have a fancy new coffee maker that the congregation gave me last Christmas. I can make whatever you prefer, espresso, latte, you name it."

"Thanks, but I usually drink plain ordinary coffee." Jack grinned. "The stronger, the better."

"I can make that, too. Call me anytime."

"Thanks." Jack waited while Grace greeted almost everyone in the congregation. When they were finally in her car, he said, "Your minister sure is a friendly fellow."

"Yes, he is. He also likes to show off his coffee machine." Grace's laughter rang merrily through the vehicle.

Jack loved the sound of it, like pure joy set free. And how had he never noticed how her smile lit her entire face? Or had he simply forgotten?

"Pastor Ed loves coffee, any kind of coffee," Grace told him. "Our ladies' group decided it would be the perfect Christmas gift for him. And it was."

The way she said that made him ask, "But?"

"He got the whole thing set up in his office, bought some cups and other stuff to go with it, and had a cute little bistro kind of thing going." Gracie giggled again.

"You're deliberately stretching this out," he accused, charmed by her sideways smirk.

"I am because it's just too funny. All that anticipation and preparation, people in his office waiting and—the machine wouldn't work," she said with another chortle. "The thing was defective. He had to wait an entire six weeks for it to be replaced. The whole time he was like a kid who finally gets the Christmas toy he's spent ages dreaming about, but when he does, it won't work. He was almost inconsolable."

"And now that he has it?" Jack asked, mostly to keep her talking. He could listen to Gracie talk forever.

"He can't stop inviting others to share it." She shook her head ruefully. "His wife told us he's begun ordering his coffee by the case, just to make sure he doesn't run out."

"Hmm. Sounds like maybe he needs a study about addictions." Jack wasn't sure what he'd said to make Gracie burst into new peals of laughter.

"He did try to quit," she explained. "He made a big cover for the machine. Out of sight, out of mind, right?"

"And?" Jack had never indulged in a lot of chit-chat. But he was enjoying this, enjoying Gracie's amusement. Even Lizzie seemed entranced by her story.

"S-someone gave him some special tea for his birthday." She pulled into a parking spot at the local pizza place and slapped a hand over her mouth. "S-sorry," she said when her laughter died down. But there was no way she could mask her lingering delight in the story. "When Ed realized he could brew hot water for his tea with his machine, off came the cover. Now he offers his guests tea and coffee in a multitude of varieties. He has so many kinds he can drink it 'til the cows come home."

"Well, he'll probably tire of it." Jack opened the door and asked Lizzie to hand him his crutches.

"Not so far." Gracie's smile stretched from ear to ear. "His latest thing is iced coffee and tea."

"Okay," Jack said thoughtfully. "Doesn't seem he could take it much further though."

"You don't think so?" She held the door for him and Lizzie to go through, a glint in her eyes that told him he didn't know the whole story yet.

"Come on, what's the rest of it?" While they waited for the hostess, he nudged her.

"The rodeo we're planning at the Double H?" Grace watched him.

"Yes. What about—oh." He frowned. "But how?"

"Nobody knows. Him opening a coffee booth at the rodeo is part two in Pastor Ed's coffee-machine saga," she said merrily before following their host to a table. "Stay tuned."

"What does Miss P. mean, Pops?" Lizzie slid into the booth beside him.

"It means that there's no end to the story, Sweet Pea. Not yet." Jack smiled at Gracie, suddenly aware that there was no place he'd rather be than right here. If only he'd brought along his camera to capture these moments forever.

"You're where?" Grace blinked when Jess said she was going to bask on a beach in Fiji. She quickly checked the travel calendar she'd created on her phone when she'd planned to take her trip, amazed by how little she'd thought about it. "Mercy! How the time has passed. It's almost May."

"Flown for me, too," Jess agreed. "I'll send you some pictures later when I can use the port's WiFi. This has been such a wonderful trip. What are you doing? Married yet?" her friend teased.

"No. And not likely to be," she groused, feeling her irritation at Jack rise again.

"Uh oh. Want to talk about it?" Jess sounded

worried so Grace changed gears, unwilling to douse her friend's joy.

"Nothing to say, really. Anyway, I'll manage," she temporized in a brighter tone.

"*Manage?* How tepid that sounds." Jess remained silent for a moment before asking, "How's Lizzie?"

"We're getting along very well. She's due home from school soon. She's such a lovely girl, but she's still not as carefree as I'd like. I haven't managed to get her to talk about her loss either." She poked the half-hearted stems on her dying flowers and knew it was time to let them go, the same as it was time to let go of the hope that something could rekindle between her and Jack.

"You sound defeated, Grace."

"I guess I am a bit," she admitted, but quickly added, "I'm not sure I know how to help Lizzie, Jess. She retreats to her bedroom a lot. Jack says she looks at the pictures of her parents on her tablet."

"Why don't you get her someplace where she can't hide out? Get her talking. You're good at that." Jess was silent a moment before she asked, "Do Ben and Bonnie still have their meadow?"

"Yes." Grace felt a flush of warmth infuse her heart. "Actually, Jack picked—never mind."

"What aren't you saying, friend of mine?" Jess's amusement transmitted clearly. "Are you falling for your former love?"

"Jack was never that, and no, I'm not." But she couldn't stop thinking about him. "What were you saying about Peace Meadow?"

"Why don't you take Lizzie there? You could have a picnic or a wiener roast or something. If no one else was around she'd be free to unload if she wants to. Oh, here comes my shave ice. My, it's huge!"

"The meadow is a great idea, Jess. Thank you." Grace smiled at the thought of her friend allowing sunshine to touch her pale, white, always-protected skin. "Now go enjoy your treat and rest up for your next big adventure. Bye, dear. I love you."

"I love you, too, Grace." And then Jess was gone.

Grace had no sooner ended the call when her phone rang again.

"Hello, Grace," Ben thundered. "Just wondering if you were all right over there."

"I'm fine, Ben. Why would you think otherwise?" she asked in some surprise.

"I wouldn't. It's Jack. He was all hot and bothered because you missed the meeting this afternoon. The rodeo meeting," he clarified. When Grace didn't immediately respond, he repeated her name.

"I'm sorry, Ben. I completely forgot. It's been a bit of a trying day and—"

"You didn't miss much. Just preliminary stuff

like planning the date. First weekend in July, by the way. I told Jack I'm sure you'll get up to speed quickly at the next one."

"Which will be?" Grace held her pen poised, ready.

"We're thinking Monday, but we'll text to confirm," he promised.

"Monday would be perfect for me. Thank you so much, Ben."

"By the way, Jack tried to call you a couple of times but couldn't get through. He asked me to tell you he's going out with the chuck wagon and will have supper on the trail with the crew."

"Oh." Grace's heart sank. Poor Lizzie. Dinner without her 'Pops.' Again.

"We're feeding a trekking group who're doing a hike, ten miles out, ten miles back," Ben explained. "I doubt Jack will be back before nine-thirty or so."

"All right, thanks for telling me, Ben, though I don't know why Jack couldn't have texted me himself." *Because he didn't want you to stop him.*

"He was in a hurry, I guess. Bye now, Grace." Ben hung up.

Grace sighed, troubled that Jack would once again be absent for Lizzie's bedtime, for the third time this week. Was he avoiding Lizzie? Or was it her he wanted to get away from?

Her phone pinged as Jess's pictures began arriving. So pretty. So carefree. Grace sent a text but then her thoughts returned to the child she was trying to help. Last night when Jack hadn't come to see her, his granddaughter had gone to bed early without even asking Grace to hear her prayers.

It was time to get Lizzie talking, but it was also way past time to have a heart-to-heart with Jack. Naturally he was engaged in ranch affairs. They offered an interest when his injured leg made it hard to do much else. Then a little voice inside her brain made Grace wonder if Jack wasn't avoiding Lizzie in an attempt to avoid responsibility.

The question was—why?

She didn't like considering that, but neither could she shed the feeling that this grandfather wanted to shift some of his obligations onto her. Understandable, of course, because being Lizzie's sole caregiver after her parents' deaths, as well as losing his son, had to have been devastating for Jack.

"But if that's his main motive for proposing, it's still not a good enough reason for me to marry him," she muttered to herself gloomily. "I can't be all things to Lizzie. Anyway, I'm the outsider."

Was that why God hadn't shown her a clear path to follow? Was He trying to make her understand that marriage was more than the unrealistic picture she'd held on to all these years?

Especially marriage to a man who had a grieving granddaughter he didn't know how to deal with?

"Oh fiddle!" she said in exasperation. "Maybe I should have gone on that trip. Then Jack would have had to figure things out for himself."

But she would have missed getting to know him and Lizzie.

Don't cry over cracked diamonds, Grace. Her father's voice repeated his favorite adage.

"Just clean up the mess," she finished and chuckled at her silliness. This situation wasn't exactly a mess of diamonds, but Lizzie was worth the effort.

She would deal with Jack. Eventually.

Chapter Seven

Later that day, when the last load of Lizzie's clothes was clean and stored, when the floor had been scrubbed free of a juice spill from breakfast, and after a quick vacuum of the area rug, Grace made her favorite cookies to go with the picnic she'd prepared.

She was pulling out the last cookie sheet as the school bus pulled in. A moment later Lizzie came bounding up the stairs and into the house.

"Is Pops here?" she asked hopefully.

"No, dear. He's gone with one of the chuck wagons to take supper to one of Ben's groups." Chagrined when Lizzie's happy smile faded, she added, "But you and I are in for a treat. Change out of your school clothes into your old jeans and a shirt because we might get dirty."

"Doing what?" Lizzie frowned at the backpack and small cooler sitting by the door. "I don't want to go anywhere in case Pops come back."

"Ben said Jack wouldn't be back till long after supper so we have lots of time. Let's get going," she urged cheerfully. "I need some fresh air and sunshine and we're going to have supper out."

"I better stay here in case Pops comes home early," the child offered listlessly.

"Then you'd miss everything!" Grace shook her head. "No way." *Jack, you will be hearing from me.* "I've prepared a surprise for you, dear, and we are leaving in three minutes," she insisted.

"I hafta go?" After one glance at her face, Lizzie didn't wait for a verbal response. She plodded into her room, returning a nanosecond before the three minutes had elapsed.

"Good girl," Grace applauded. "Now which would you like to carry, the cooler bag or the backpack?"

Lizzie picked up the backpack, her face expressing her utter indifference for this surprise. She remained silent as they plodded up and down the uneven path, but when she caught sight of the lovely green meadow with its gazebo, comfy chairs and the picnic table, her face brightened.

"First we'll need a fire." Grace chose newspaper, kindling and smaller sticks from the wood box and showed Lizzie how to hide the balled-up paper under tiny bits of wood. She let her hold the starter until the flame caught. Then she demonstrated the way to add chips of wood until the fire had grown enough to catch onto thin sticks and finely split logs.

"I didn't know you knew how to build a fire, Miss P.," Lizzie marveled.

"I learned at Camp Tapawingo." Grace smiled

as she sank into one of the Adirondack chairs that circled the firepit. "That was the very first year I attended."

"The place where you learned to fish?" Lizzie sat beside her as she ruminated on that. "What else did you learn there?"

"Oh, a lot of things. How to forgive friends when they hurt you. How to make new friends and help them not to be scared. And how to make s'mores," she added with a chuckle. "I'd never had them before camp and I loved them."

"They're yummy," Lizzie agreed, her voice quiet. "Did you have a good friend there?"

"Yes. Jess is still my good friend. When we were kids, she and her family lived next door. When she got married, she moved to a different house in Sunshine. But we have stayed good friends all these years." She paused before tentatively asking, "Did you have a good friend in Texas?"

"My mom. She was my best friend." Lizzie stared at her hands as tears rolled down her cheeks. "Now I don't have one."

"But you can make another friend." When Lizzie shook her head, Grace leaned forward and clasped her hand. "Listen to me, dear. Your mom will always have a very special place in your heart that nobody else can ever take. That's just how it is with moms."

The girl looked dubious but at least she was

listening. Grace let her words sink in for a few minutes before she continued.

"The thing is, Lizzie, your mom would never want you to remember her but not make another best friend. In fact, she'd *want* you to make one," Grace insisted. "More than one."

Lizzie frowned. "Why?"

"Because friends help us when the hard times come in our lives. They can share our problems and our hurts." She touched the unruly hair that refused to remain constrained by a ponytail. "Things never seem quite so bad if we have someone to share with."

"Pops tole me that when he lived in Sunshine, you an' him were friends." It was impossible to dodge Lizzie's honest inquiry, though Grace had no desire to think about the dark times she'd gone through when her relationship with Jack had ended so abruptly.

"We were very good friends," she admitted. "But he and his family moved away. That was hard for me, but I had my friend Jess to help me. Pretty soon, the hurt went away."

Not quite true, Grace, her brain chided. *It wasn't pretty soon. It took ages. If you're even over it now.* She stared into the flames, plunged into memories of sad days and feelings of loss she'd thought she would never escape.

"I'm why Pops had to sell his ranch," Lizzie burst out.

"My dear, I don't think that's true," Grace protested with a frown.

"It is so." Lizzie glared at her. "Pops told me lots of stories about Milt and how they ranched together. Even when my dad took over the ranch, Pops always came back for roundup. He loved going in the rodeos, too." She sniffed sadly. "But after—you know." She stopped, sniffed and then pressed on. "He couldn't keep ranching, or rodeoing or taking pictures 'cause he had to look after me."

"You feel a bit guilty about that, don't you?" Grace exhaled when she nodded. "But I don't think you should, because I don't think your pops selling the ranch was only because he had to look after you."

"Huh?" Lizzie looked confused.

"Do you remember the times when your pops would go away from the ranch?" Grace prayed she was handling this right.

"Yeah. Sometimes he didn't come back for a long time." Her wistful tone faded. "But then he'd stay an' we'd have fun and go riding and go fishing. But we couldn't do that no more when my mom an' dad died 'cause Pops had too much work to do. 'Cause he loved ranching," she added very quietly.

More than me, was implicit in her words. Grace couldn't let that pass.

"Do you know why your pops went away all

those times, dear?" She watched Lizzie's frown reappear. After a moment's contemplation, she shook her head.

"I think I do and it has nothing to do with you."

Lizzie stared at her in disbelief. "How do *you* know that?"

"When Jack lived in Sunshine, way back when I knew him," she added with a smile. "He loved to do one thing. Can you guess what it was?"

"I dunno. He likes taking pictures," Lizzie said uncertainly.

"No. He *loves* taking pictures." Grace chuckled. "I'd forgotten that until we started talking about camp and I remembered that's where Jack first learned about photography. After we came home from camp, he wanted a camera so badly that he agreed to work for his dad in the church so he could get enough money to buy one."

"He did? But my dad tole me Pops an' his daddy had bad fights," Lizzie asserted, nose scrunched up in disbelief.

"They did," Grace agreed. "Maybe because Jack didn't understand what his father was trying to teach him about God. I think that's why he likes taking pictures. I think they help him see things differently."

"Sometimes I don't understand 'bout God," Lizzie mumbled.

"Neither do I sometimes, dear," she explained before Lizzie could ask. "But we *can* understand that we are His children and that He loves us and will take care of us, always."

"You mean God loved me even when He made my mommy an' daddy die?" Lizzie's stark question floored Grace, but it demanded an answer.

"I don't believe God *made* them die," she said carefully. "But I do believe that God loves you and is always working to make things better for you. God's love never changes. He will always love us, no matter what."

"Huh." Lizzie watched the fire for a while, puzzling it through until her stomach rumbled.

"I think we'd better cook our supper now." Grace tickled her. "Before your stomach gets louder. It sounds angry," she teased.

"It is 'cause I didn't eat all my lunch today," Lizzie admitted while Grace helped her thread a smoked sausage onto one of the metal forks that were tucked in a nearby storage box.

"Why didn't you?" Grace wondered.

"This kid, Marcus. He said his mom was at work an' his dad was asleep an' nobody made him lunch, an' then the bus came an'—" Lizzie shrugged. "So anyway, I shared mine."

"That was very kind of you." Grace squeezed her shoulder. "Exactly the kind of thing God wants His children to do, share with one another."

"No biggie." Lizzie shared some details of her life pre-Sunshine that gave Grace a clearer picture of the child's troubling insecurities.

Lizzie didn't feel she fit anywhere anymore. Perhaps having her and Jack stay at the Double H wasn't a good idea because eventually, Lizzie would have another home, another place to fit into. Grace encouraged the child to talk some more, but it wasn't long before Lizzie grew more interested in the trunk of toys than talking. Then they played games.

As late afternoon turned into evening and shadows began to fall, Grace reluctantly packed up their things. She showed Lizzie how to flatten the few coals that were left, place the cover on top and check that everything was stored ready for the next user. Then they started home.

"Do you think Pops will be there?" Lizzie's hopeful tone hurt to hear.

"I doubt it, dear. Ben said he'd be late." An idea hit. "Lizzie, just because your pops isn't always nearby, and because he gets caught up taking pictures, that doesn't mean he doesn't love you. Your pops does love you very much. He's not going to leave you."

"He might," Lizzie whispered as they climbed the last hill. "He might get sick and die. God might want that."

"Well, I suppose it's possible." Grace agreed very softly. She stopped where she was and smoothed a hand over Lizzie's dark hair. "But I don't believe God wants that at all. I think God made sure your grandfather was there when you really needed him and that He'll keep him with you so you won't be alone. Because God loves you very much, Lizzie, dear."

While Lizzie prepared for bed, Grace stored their used items from the cooler and hung the backpack in the closet, praying silently for knowledge to help this troubled child. When nothing came to mind, she picked up the storybook she always read to Lizzie before bed and wondered which Biblical tale would be most suitable for tonight.

"I like that book." Lizzie stood in the doorway, her scrubbed face aglow in the light. "If we're reading from it again, I wanna hear the story about the boy who looked after sheep an' God made him king."

"David," Grace said automatically. She patted the seat beside her and waited until Lizzie was curled up there. "Why that story?"

"'Cause it makes me think about him not having his daddy or mommy to help him when he had to run away from the other king, an' how he did okay." Lizzie picked at a loose thread on the cushion she hugged against herself. "I want to be like him, but I miss my mommy and daddy," she whispered.

"I know you do, dear." Grace's heart ached for this sweet child and all she'd lost. "I'm sure you did lots of fun things with them, didn't you?"

"Yes!" She lifted her chin and met Grace's gaze

with a sad face. "But I can't 'member everything. Sometimes I can't even 'member their faces." She burst into tears.

That's why you keep looking at your tablet.

Grace knew it was true. She also knew she had to do something. Lizzie was hurting. Since Jack wasn't here, it was up to her to fix things. But how? She eased the book out of the way so she could fold Lizzie into an embrace and that's when the second idea came.

"Listen to me now, child." She tenderly brushed away the tears and smiled into that small sorrowful face. "You haven't really forgotten your parents. Their faces are just tucked away for now, because there's too much to remember all at once."

"But I want to remember everything!" Lizzie wailed.

"I know." Grace squeezed her hand. "I might have an idea how to do that. Do you want to hear it?"

"Y-yes." The child sniffed so loudly that it was impossible to begin without first handing her a tissue to blow her nose.

"I think you need to have a special book," she said gently. "Some of the Calhoun children who lived in Africa and had to leave their home made one and it helped them."

"How can a book—"

"Books can do a lot of things, Lizzie. I should

know. I was a librarian for many years and I've watched lots of people find the help they need in books." Grace smiled at the inquisitive face and realized she truly enjoyed the moments of sharing with this child.

"We gotta read a book to 'member Mommy and Daddy better?" Lizzie frowned. "O-okay, but where do I get a book about my mommy and daddy?"

"I meant you should *make* a book." She watched the idea percolate through the girl's mind.

"I dunno how to make books!" Lizzie exclaimed.

"It's quite easy. Every time you think of a fun time you and your parents shared, you either paint or draw a picture in your book to remind you. I'm sure your pops has pictures of your parents—"

"Yup, he does. An' if he gives me some, I could put 'em in the book. Like the time we went on a sleigh ride into the woods to get our Christmas tree!" Lizzie's excitement created a huge smile that engaged her entire face. "An' like the first day I went to school."

"And perhaps when you learned to ride your horse?" She strove to sound matter-of-fact. Riding had apparently been important to Lizzie at one time. "I heard you had white boots. I'd love to see a picture of those." Grace recalled when she'd first learned to ride right here on the Double H, just a few years ago. "I used to have red boots."

"I don't want to make no pictures about riding," Lizzie said with a firm shake of her head. "But I c'n make other pictures. Maybe that kind of a book would make me not so lonely," she whispered to herself.

The child had isolated herself for so long that she probably now found it more difficult to interact with anyone but her Pops. School was helping, but Lizzie needed more.

"Are you lonely a lot, dear?" Grace asked in a very gentle tone.

"Sometimes I am. That's when I go to my room." She glanced over one shoulder, as if to ensure no one could overhear. Her voice dropped. "Pops doesn't know it, but I look on my tablet at the newspaper story 'bout them when I need to 'member their faces."

The story about her parents' deaths? Appalled, Grace tucked her forefinger under that determined chin and forced Lizzie's amber eyes to meet hers.

"Tomorrow you must show me, dear. Then we'll get rid of those sad pictures and put happy ones in their place. And we'll start your book. Maybe we can use some pictures your pops took." She frowned. "It's not healthy to look at sad things all the time, Lizzie."

"'Cause it makes you more sadder." Lizzie nodded. "I know. When can we get a book for me to put my pictures in?"

"We can drive to town on Saturday morning. Your pops will come with us," Grace said firmly. She pressed her lips together and shook her head when Lizzie suggested he might have other plans. "No, dear," she said firmly, "I'm very sure your pops wants to spend Saturday with you, doing fun things."

"Sure?" Lizzie asked hesitantly.

"Positive." *Don't you even think about arguing with me, Jack Prinz*, she warned mentally. "Then you'll be able to draw a picture of our happy times for your book, too. We'll get a huge book with lots of pages and lovely colored pencils or crayons, whichever you like."

"What if it gets full?" the little girl wondered.

"Full of happy memories?" Grace laughed. "Why then we'll get another one and fill it up, too." She touched the hunched shoulder. "And when you can't remember your mom and dad or the fun times you had together, we'll take out your books and look at them and they will remind you of such happy times."

"Okay." Lizzie smiled to herself at the thought of it. "Can we have the story about that boy now?" she asked after a huge yawn.

"Yes, we surely can, dear."

Grace read with great expression, reminding herself that this was no different than the many occasions she'd read for preschoolers and school groups during story time at the library. But tonight, she took extra care to make the story as lifelike as possible for the little girl. She sometimes forgot Lizzie was not quite six because she always seemed old for her years. Perhaps grief and being alone so much had caused her to grow up quickly. Well, tonight she was going to go to bed with happy dreams about a boy who became a king.

She took her time tucking Lizzie into bed, ensuring she was no longer sad, and that a tiny nightlight burned lest she become frightened in the night.

"Sweet dreams, Lizzie," she murmured tenderly, brushing a kiss against her velvety cheek. "Dream about all the happy things we'll do together."

"Us and Pops," Lizzie agreed, her eyelids drooping. "Night, Miss P."

Never had Grace's longing to be called an endearment risen so strong. But that wasn't happening so she'd just have to make do by showering her love on Lizzie. And that meant involving her grandfather.

"There is no way that child is going to spend another moment alone in her room, staring at an ugly newspaper report just so she can remind herself of her parents' faces," Grace promised herself as she stepped onto the deck to enjoy the night air and the first star's appearance. "Not on my watch."

She purposely didn't turn on a light. Sometimes the gloom of anonymity was needed to aid in organizing thoughts. She got lost thinking about Jack and wondering what things had happened to him to turn him into who he was, which was why she was still sitting there when the chuck wagon appeared and the driver let "Pops" off at the main house. Jack limped toward the door, paused and turned to glance at the log cabin.

Come over here, her mind begged. *Come check on your granddaughter. She needs to see you. So do I, Jack. Talk to me. See me as more than Lizzie's caregiver. I need to be more to you than a handy convenience. I need so much more from you. Please, think about me.*

But Jack mustn't have heard or sensed her pleas, because after a moment's scrutiny, he shrugged, turned and entered the main house.

Grace straightened her shoulders.

All right then. If he couldn't see it for himself, she'd have to show him that neither she nor Lizzie was going to be cast aside. It was time Jack learned about real partnership, the kind needed if a marriage was to happen, though right now Grace was highly doubtful he could be the partner she needed. God would have to work wonders on both of them.

"Have a good sleep, Jack, because things are going to change in your world. They're going to change a lot come Saturday."

* * *

Jack's aching leg meant he usually slept fit-fully, waking often, as if there was something he'd forgotten to do. Friday night, after finally taking a second pain pill, oblivion came in the wee hours.

And was abruptly shattered Saturday morning when someone frantically pounded on his door at the crack of dawn.

"Yeah," he managed, dragging his head from the pillow.

"Sorry to wake you, Jack, but Grace Partridge just called. She asked me to tell you she'll pick you up in twenty minutes," Ben explained.

Why couldn't he get his bleary vision to clear? And why would Grace be calling him at this time of day?

"Emergency?" he grunted, struggling upright. "Lizzie?"

"She said they're fine," Ben reassured him.

"Oh." He flopped back onto his pillow. "It's Saturday, isn't it? Why does she need to pick me up?" What was the woman up to now?

"No clue. Guess you could call her and find out," Ben suggested half-heartedly. "But if I were in your shoes, I wouldn't. Grace doesn't take kindly to folks not falling in with her plans. She clearly has some for today and apparently they include you." He waited a minute then urged, "Better get up now."

Jack couldn't quite smother his groan. He dearly wanted to roll over and go back to sleep, but that wasn't going to happen. For one thing, he was now wide awake. For another, Ben was right; Grace wouldn't allow it. He forced himself to rise and prepare for the day. He managed to grab his camera and get to the kitchen one minute before his almost fiancée pushed through the back door. Just enough time to pour himself a cup of Bonnie's delicious black coffee.

"Good morning, Jack. You won't need that," Grace said cheerfully.

"Believe me, I do," he grumped, inhaling the dark aroma as if he was in the desert.

"You can have all the coffee you want at the restaurant," she chided as she lifted the mug from his hand and emptied it down the drain.

"Hey, I wanted— What restaurant?" he demanded with a frown.

"The one you're taking us to for breakfast. Come on, Jack. Lizzie's waiting in the car. We have a full day planned."

"We do? Great." He infused as much enthusiasm into the words as he was capable of, which wasn't much. Since Grace didn't move from in front of the coffee pot, he was forced to step past her out the door. He got in the car, despite his misgivings about this trip.

"Hi, Pops." Lizzie sounded happy. That was

good. Grace was good for her. Way better than he was.

"Hey, Sweet Pea." He swallowed his irritation with Grace as he folded himself into the seat, right after he'd spied a new ding on her car's bumper. Thank goodness she hadn't asked to take his vehicle wherever they were going!

"Don't you dare blame that mark on my driving," Grace chided as she slipped into the driver's seat. "Mordecai Miller backed into me at the post office. Honestly, that man is so cheap. He refuses to buy himself new glasses, though he's needed them for at least two years."

"Uh-huh." Given the glower from her pansy eyes, Jack skipped commenting and focused on his granddaughter. "How are you, darlin'?"

"I'm okay." Lizzie's smile faded. "You didn't come and say good-night to me for lotsa nights, Pops."

"No, sorry. I've been getting back pretty late. All the lights were off at your place so I didn't want to bother you." It was a shabby excuse and he knew it, but the shots he'd taken after dark, of the starlit sky with no human lights to impede, were going to be glorious. He changed the subject. "We're going out for breakfast, huh? Good. You can tell me what you've been up to."

"Me an' Miss P. have been really busy. We're gonna make a book today. Well, I'm makin' it and she's helpin'," Lizzie corrected. "An' you're helpin' us, too, Pops."

"I am? Making a book?" Jack gaped at Grace. "*You're* the librarian. I know nothing about making books."

"So you'll learn." She half smiled. "I'll teach you. But for now, let's think about what we're going to enjoy for breakfast." Grace briskly turned the corner onto the highway, cutting it a bit short so they spit gravel.

Jack, leg throbbing, tightened his grip on his seat belt.

"I believe I'll have waffles with fresh strawberries and whipped cream," she continued as if nothing was amiss. "Lizzie, what would you like?"

"Pancakes and blueberry syrup," his granddaughter asserted. "What are you havin', Pops?"

"Cackleberries, overland trout, some wasp nest, maybe." He smothered a grin at Grace's wide-eyed glance.

"Don'tcha want any hash browns?" Lizzie asked. "You always have hash browns, Pops."

"Not that hungry today," Jack explained, and then added rather smugly, "That's eggs, bacon and bread, preferably sourdough, to you, Gracie."

"Thanks for the translation, but I understand most cowboy lingo. I did some research on it for a town project a few years ago." She ignored him to chat with Lizzie the rest of the way into town.

Slightly miffed that he hadn't bested her, Jack felt excluded from their conversation. But though he wanted to interrupt, he couldn't think of anything to say, mostly because he wasn't up on what they'd been doing.

He should be. He admitted the truth to himself with a touch of chagrin. It was just that it had been so long since he'd had full days to himself to shoot whatever photos he wanted. Maybe he could play catch-up over breakfast.

"Here's the plan for today, Jack," Gracie explained after they'd ordered. "We have a bit of shopping to do."

"More shopping? What more could the child possibly need to wear?" he asked.

"Not to wear, to eat," Grace said briskly. "We're running low on groceries, Jack. Since we're in town, we'll stock up."

"An' get the book," Lizzie reminded. "We hafta get that."

"Yes, we sure do." Grace shared a tender smile with her that made Jack feel even more left out. "We'll return our books to the library and pick up some fresh reading and then we'll take a run to Middlebrook."

"Where?" Jack asked, already tired by the schedule.

"It's about half an hour away. There's something there that might work for the kids' rodeo at the Double H. I want Lizzie to check it out with me. Now, what else?" She opened her bag and tugged out her phone, consulting it for several moments before nodding. "Oh, yes. And that. We must do that."

"Must we?" he asked mournfully.

"Honestly, Jack, you're like a wet blanket this morning. Oh, here's our food." Grace smiled widely at their server as she set their meals before them. She accepted more coffee for both of them and then gave thanks for the food. She picked up her fork only to pause and frown at him. "Drink your coffee. Perhaps a delicious breakfast and a day in the fresh air will refresh you," she said. "If not, I suppose you can rest in the car during the drive to Middlebrook."

He felt as if she'd just aged him by ten years and Lizzie didn't help matters.

"Maybe Pops needs a nap." She giggled as if it was a great joke.

"Maybe I do," Jack agreed grimly. But seeing Grace's smirk made him determined to outlast them both. After breakfast, their search for the drawing book Lizzie kept talking about confused him. "She doesn't have to draw anything. I have photos, Gracie. Lots of them," he told her in a low tone while his granddaughter sorted through the available stock in the general store. "I have albums, too."

"Lizzie needs to make her own book," Grace insisted. "She needs the process." He didn't understand that, but he got that it *was* going to happen when she added, "Of course, I'm sure she'd love some of your pictures to go in it also."

The way she said that annoyed him. As if they were some second-rate shots taken by an amateur! His pictures were primo.

Jack had never heard Gracie be deliberately unkind to anyone and maybe she hadn't meant to be denigrating. But he was still getting the strongest impression that she was irritated with him for something. The reason why was a mystery, but he was pretty sure Grace would reveal the clues before the end of the day.

He deserved whatever she said. He'd wanted a champion for Lizzie and Grace was exactly that. But he wondered. Would she ever be a champion for him?

And why would he want her to be?

Chapter Eight

"I have to hand it to you, Grace. Coming here was an awesome idea."

Jack paused in his photo shoot of Lizzie to beam at her. Grace felt the telltale rush of color in her cheeks and quickly swerved her gaze away from him, pretending to study his granddaughter as she cooed and petted the Shetland ponies who lived on a small ranch just outside Middlebrook. She basked in his compliment.

"I'm glad you approve. I thought these folks might agree to bring a couple of their ponies to our rodeo to entertain children not participating in the events. I know you're anxious for Lizzie to ride again," she added hurriedly. "But there's something blocking her from doing that. I've encouraged her in several ways, but she refuses to even discuss the possibility of riding, as well as anything that goes with it. Like those new boots," she reminded.

"Which she rejected. So, you thought getting her to remember riding at our ranch by petting these ponies and making that book you both talk about would help." He nodded approvingly. "Good plan."

"But that's not what I thought at all!" Why couldn't he understand that forcing things was not a solution?

"Then?" He glanced from Lizzie to her, his face a question mark.

"I want your granddaughter to explore her feelings, to figure out in her own way, and her own time, why she doesn't want to continue doing something she once enjoyed." Grace saw he still didn't get it. "Lizzie's struggling to work out her place in this new world she's in, Jack. I think her feelings have to do with abandonment, or something like that, but—"

"She wasn't abandoned!" Jack huffed, obviously irritated as his eyes darkened with fury. "I'm right here."

"Listen to *me* now, Pops," Grace insisted. She laid her hand on his arm for fear he'd stomp away in anger before hearing what she had to say. "First, let's take you and your feelings out of this equation."

"But—"

"No buts. This isn't about you, Jack. Or me. It's all about Lizzie. Whether you think her issues make sense or not is irrelevant. It's what *she* feels that matters." She lifted her hand away and let it drop to her side because the warm tingles emanating from touching him were too strong. "Anyway," she said soothingly. "I didn't say abandonment *was* her issue. I said it *could* be. Or it may be something else. The point is, we need to find out."

Jack thought about it for a moment, his gaze resting on the laughing girl who was enjoying the ponies as they snatched bits of carrot from her palm. He took several more shots to add to the hundred or so he'd already taken before finally letting his camera hang around his neck. He huffed a sigh of resignation as his gaze met and locked with Grace's.

"I'll give it some thought." He pointed to a nearby bench, and when she nodded, began walking toward it.

"Better?" she guessed when he exhaled as he sank onto the metal.

"Much." Jack turned so he was facing her. "How do you do it, Gracie?"

Would he ever drop that tired old nickname? Ever see her for who she really was, a woman and not some ingenuous young girl, overwhelmed by his charm? She had so much more to offer.

"How do I do what?" Under the watchful eye of the owner, Lizzie was leading one of the ponies around the paddock. When Jack didn't answer immediately, Grace turned her focus on him. "What are you asking?"

"How do you find a way to help so many people with their problems?" He chuckled at her eye roll. "I know you do exactly that. Staying at the

Double H means I'm learning lots about you, Gracie."

"Such as?" Did she *want* Jack to know more about her? But that was inevitable if she was going to marry him. *Was* she going to marry him?

"Yesterday, when I was watching Ben saddle break a colt, one of the hands, Oliver, told me how you helped him figure out some things in his faith life. He spoke very highly of you, Gracie. So did another guy called Mark who said you helped straighten out his love life." Jack smiled smugly.

"I did no such thing!" Grace scowled with distaste, then frowned suspiciously. "Are you making fun of me?"

"Not in the least." Jack lifted her hand and entwined his fingers with hers, his smile gentle. "More like I'm totally amazed and impressed that you've become so skilled at helping folks figure out how to make their lives better. Ben's told me stories about how you got the whole town working together on a Christmas project to raise money to fix the town hall."

"Sam did most of that. I just helped," she corrected as tingles rose up her arm from his touch.

"Yeah, Sam told me exactly how much you 'helped.'" Jack's golden eyes twinkled when he squeezed her hand. She enjoyed the thrill of it for a moment more before she tugged free of his grasp.

"You make me sound like a busybody." Grace paused and wondered, was she?

"You might be a busybody, but not in a negative way." Jack looked out across the acres of rolling pasture. "Sometimes you remind me of my mom."

Since Jack had always spoken very fondly of his mother, Grace assumed this was a compliment. But she wanted to know more about the woman he'd loved.

"Remind you how?" Grace was half-afraid to hear his answer.

"Well, as a pastor's wife, I'm sure she knew many details about people, things they might not want others to know. I never knew her to counsel anyone, but she did keep her eyes and ears open and took note of what was happening around her, of people who were hurt, needed support or some other kind of assistance. And she almost always found some way to help them. Not that most people knew because she never said a word."

"Your mother was very perceptive," Grace agreed, reminded of the "chance" meeting she'd had with Jack's mother just before his family had moved. Mrs. Prinz's quiet advice to seek God's healing for her hurting heart had stuck with Grace for a long time.

"Mom often spoke about you." His voice softened when he turned his head. His gaze meshed with hers so intensely that she couldn't break the connection. "You do the same things as she did, in your own way. You have an impact on people, Gracie. For good."

"Well, thank you, Jack," she murmured, uncomfortable yet deeply moved by his praise. "I don't really try to get involved you know. But when someone needs help and I know about it, well—"

"You can't walk away." He nodded. "That's because you have an amazing gift of seeing a need and finding a way to fill it." He grimaced. "I never got that gene."

Though thrilled by his praise, Grace was more concerned with Jack's self-deprecation. She sent a silent prayer before responding.

"It isn't a gene one inherits, Jack. It's a—a training," she said after struggling to find the right word. "Something you teach yourself. When you notice needs or things you could change, then you try to figure out how to make that happen. Then you do it again. And again. After a while it comes naturally." She shrugged. "My parents lived that way so if I'm the same, I guess I picked it up from them."

"Your dad used to notice if kids needed new shoes or a bigger winter coat," Jack remembered, his expression thoughtful. "Or even if somebody just needed a break. He took me for lunch once when I was having a tough time. I can still taste that milkshake and burger." He made a face.

"Though I'm afraid I don't recall his words of wisdom to help correct whatever misdeed I'd committed that day. I just remember it felt like somebody cared about me."

Somebody cared about me. Oh, Jack, her heart sighed.

"Dad never fussed much about misdeeds," Grace said softly. "He was more concerned about a person's heart."

"Yeah." Jack's soft smile told her he was recalling some of her dad's other actions. Then he laughed, a happy, musical sound in the bucolic setting. "I also remember several occasions when my mom and yours would meet to discuss organizing a bake sale, though I was never too clear on their goals for the funds they raised." He thought about it for a few moments. "Seems to me that on one occasion little John Deck had a new ski suit not long after a pie sale."

"Oh, those pie sales!" Grace chuckled in memory. "I wonder how many apples I peeled for them. And now, our ladies' group has carried on the tradition, though not so much with pies."

"What do you do with the funds your group raises?" he asked curiously.

"We keep our eyes and ears open and look for ways we can minister to others without being too obvious. We always have a list of needs we're working to fill," she said airily.

"And now the rodeo. But you don't want to

talk about the other ways?" he guessed, one eyebrow arched.

"Well, it's touchy, so no. With the rodeo we can be more open because it's for the good of every kid who goes to camp. No one will be ashamed or embarrassed by our fund-raising plans for it." Grace blinked. "I hope not anyway."

"And it's easier for everyone to participate if they don't have to take the whole responsibility for fund-raising," he said thoughtfully. "When I mentioned a few ideas—" Jack stopped and studied her with a frown. "You missed the meeting again."

"Yes, I did." She pressed her lips together, unwilling to shatter the relative camaraderie they'd just shared.

"But I thought you were committed to helping. Why weren't you there?" he pressed, his forehead furrowed.

"Because, as I've already told you, there were some other things going on that I had to deal with." Since Lizzie was now walking toward them, Grace cut her comments short. She'd harken back to this discussion when they had undisturbed privacy.

"Those ponies are so sweet," Lizzie enthused. She looked like a different child with her sparkling eyes and pretty smile. Her feet almost danced as she swung herself round and round. "I love them."

"Are you going to—"

"I'm so glad you had fun." Grace had no compunction about cutting Jack off midsentence. He would *not* nag this child about riding.

Marybelle Matthews walked up to them.

"I think other kids would like to see those ponies also. They'll be a great addition to our rodeo, *if* you'll bring them?" Grace added, directing the question to the smiling owner.

"I think we can." Marybelle pulled out her phone, noted the date Grace gave her. "Yes, that works." She then bent to talk to Lizzie. "Have you some ideas about ways we could make it more fun for the kids?"

"Your ponies should have bows in their manes," the little girl said. "And you could braid their tails. Then they'd look more, um, happy," she decided.

"Good idea. And if you think of anything else, you let Grace know and she'll tell me," Marybelle insisted. "Thanks for feeding them, sweetie. They loved it."

"It was fun." Lizzie shook her hand in a very adult fashion, then stood by her grandfather. As they walked toward Grace's car, she said, "I would like a drink. And some lunch. Can we, please?"

"After all that breakfast you put away, Sweet Pea?" Jack teased, tugging on the ponytail Grace had worked so hard to make neat. Lizzie's eager nod made him roar with laughter. "Then I guess we'd better find someplace to feed this kid, Gracie."

"We could go home. I could make something for us," she offered thinking how much she enjoyed hearing him laugh.

"No way!" Jack shook his head firmly. "You've been cooking for Lizzie and me ever since we arrived. I think we should have a day of freedom for Gracie. Right, Lizzie?"

The little girl nodded happily and took her seat in the car. But Grace's focus remained on Jack. She hadn't seen him like this in a very long time. She really liked this carefree, boyish Jack.

Enough to marry him?

"Jack, these pictures are amazing!"

While they waited for the school bus on Monday morning, Jack had spread a variety of his photos on the picnic table. Grace's praise as she scanned them was music to his ears. His chest swelled with pride. This, at least, he hadn't messed up.

"Thanks," he said, enjoying her intense study of each one. "Which is your favorite?"

"It's hard to choose and even harder to explain what it is that draws me." Grace bent forward for a better look at the three she'd edged away from the others. "Essentially these are all sunsets and grazing horses. And yet there's something about each that distinguishes it from its neighbor."

She sounded puzzled so Jack explained, his hand brushing hers as he spread out the shots. Her fragrance was something light, yet slightly heady. Lilacs, maybe?

"It's all in the focus of the shot. In this one we see the twilight peeking through the clouds. But this one," he said, selecting another picture, "is more about the shadows."

"And this one." Grace pointed to the third. "This a combination of the two, but centered on showing the woods and the light's effect on them?" She glanced at him for confirmation, her eyes searching his quizzically.

"Exactly," he said with a nod.

"You know." Grace picked up one of the pictures, glanced from it to Jack and set it aside. "You have a number of pictures of the Double H like this one that would be perfect to use in our pamphlet to advertise the rodeo."

"Sure, we could use them." Jack was pleased she'd said what he'd been thinking. They thought alike. "Though I'd like to be acknowledged. Maybe something like Photos by Jack Prinz in tiny print at the bottom?"

"Of course." A noise drew Grace's attention. "Lizzie, that's the bus. Do you have your lunch?"

"Yep." Lizzie was already shouldering her

backpack. "Bye, Pops." She blew him a kiss. "Bye, Miss P."

"Goodbye, dear. Have a good day," Grace called as Lizzie went racing across the grass. Her heavy sigh made Jack frown.

"What's that for?" he asked as he gathered the pictures. He looked at her more closely and noticed there were circles under her eyes, too.

"Oh, nothing." Grace poured them fresh coffee from the carafe, probably to avoid his scrutiny.

"Gracie?" Something was going on in that beautiful head and Jack wanted to know what it was.

"It's really nothing." When he cleared his throat, she shrugged. "It's just that sometimes lately I feel a bit like I'm living with a whirlwind and I'm worried I won't be able to keep up." Her movements did seem slow as she carried the basket with their dirty breakfast dishes to the deck stairs. "I'll be fine," she quickly added.

"You don't have to do as much with her as you do, you know," he chided. "Sit and enjoy your coffee for a few minutes. You deserve a break. Let's talk."

Grace chose one of the comfy Adirondack chairs without comment. But when she was seated under the aspen tree, she studied him with a look that revealed apprehension.

"What do you want to talk about?"

"Is it too much for you, having Lizzie, staying with her, watching her all the time?" As Jack studied her lovely face, he saw something flicker in the purple depths of her eyes, something that worried him. Doubt. "You know I can find someone to stay with her after school, so you'll have some freedom."

To Jack's astonishment, his words were a flame to Gracie's tinder.

"What Lizzie does *not* need is yet another person to get used to!" Whatever meaning was behind her words, he didn't understand it and wanted to ask more. He was frustrated when whatever else she'd been about to say was bitten off by the ring of her phone. "Hello?"

Jack unabashedly eavesdropped on Gracie's conversation. Judging by the way she hedged her words she was trying to get out of whatever had been asked. But her caller was persistent.

"Of course, if there is no one else then I'll do it." She sounded resigned. "But I can only stay until noon. I have a commitment this afternoon."

Their rodeo meeting was today, Jack remembered. But that wasn't scheduled until four.

"I'll be there in about half an hour," Grace promised before ending the call.

"Is there anything I can help you with?" Jack offered, thinking he'd never seen Gracie less enthused about helping.

"It's kind of you to offer, but unless you're willing to babysit at church, no, thanks." Grace made a face as she tucked her phone into her pocket. "It's been so hectic lately that I forgot it's Jess's day to mind the babies for the moms-and-tots Bible study. I should have asked someone else to stand in, but since I didn't and since it seems no one else is available to help Millie Ens, I'll have to take Jess's place."

"I'm sorry." Jack didn't know what else to say, but he knew he was to blame for dumping his world on her. "Anything I could do here to help out?" He glanced around, trying to see something he could do to make her world easier, but nothing that a guy on crutches could do came to mind.

"Actually, there is something." Grace studied him with a skeptical look.

"Name it." Jack's shoulders went back. He'd show her he could handle things. Then maybe she'd be more positive about them marrying.

"Could you be here when Lizzie gets home?" She seemed to appraise him before adding, "She'll need a snack and she'll want to talk about her day."

"I thought you said you'd only work until lunch." When Grace scowled, Jack knew he was in danger of failing this test and hastily backpedaled. "Sure, I can do that. Sweet Pea and I will have a good chat."

"Thank you. I have a few errands I'd like to get done and it would really help if I didn't have to rush back here with some left unfinished." Grace carried their dishes inside, probably loaded them in the dishwasher, too, before coming back down the steps with her sweater in one hand and her handbag and keys in the other. One hand patted her hair.

"You look lovely, Gracie."

"Thank you." She fixed him with stern regard. "You can't forget, Jack. You *must* be here. Lizzie can't come home to an empty house. She'd be scared that something had happened." She kept a bead on him. "You won't forget, will you, Jack? This is important."

"I'll be here," he promised.

After a few more moments of intense scrutiny, Grace nodded and got in her car.

"Enjoy your morning and the babies," he called, then wished he hadn't when she twisted to give him a glance that hinted at something that she was too polite to utter.

What had he said wrong? Didn't all women enjoy babies?

Jack sat and enjoyed his coffee and the busyness of the ranch for a while. But then his leg reminded him he needed to move around. He left his cup on the table. He'd ask Lizzie to take it into the house when she came home.

The sunshine, the light breeze and the spring colts attracted him. He decided to take a little stroll around the ranch. Gracie kept saying he needed to exercise his leg. He would do what she wanted, as a good husband should.

Proud of his reasoning, Jack strolled to the main house to get his hat and met Ben, who stopped his truck and leaned out the open window to talk.

"I'm on my way out to the high country. Want to join me?" the rancher invited.

"When will you be back?" Jack wasn't going to let Gracie down, not when he'd promised.

"Bonnie's baking pies so I'll for sure be back by lunchtime," Ben assured him confidently. "Interested?"

"Sure." Slapping his Stetson on his head, Jack swung himself into the seat. He'd be back long before Lizzie came home from school. No problem.

Chapter Nine

As Grace drove onto the ranch later that afternoon, she was surprised by how welcoming she found the sight of the little log house. She'd lived in Sunshine for so long that calling anywhere else home had always seemed impossible. Until now. The Double H and this house felt like home. Why was that?

Because of Lizzie and Jack.

That thought so startled her that she sat thinking about it until the warmth of the sun made her drowsy. She forced herself to slough off her weariness and get out of the vehicle. A mere two hours of babysitting this morning hadn't caused this fatigue. Nor was it due to the odd jobs she'd just finished. Watering Jess's houseplants, weeding her garden and flower beds, mowing her lawn—she'd done it all because she wasn't certain when next she'd be able to return.

But this lethargy that held her in its grip was not due to hard work. The gnawing unease that nagged at her now and often kept her awake at night was solely due to Jack and his proposal.

Speaking of…

Grace stepped inside the house, annoyed to find the entry door ajar.

"Lizzie? Jack?"

Neither one answered, though a ranch cat blinked at her from his position on the sofa. Grace shooed him outside and closed the screen door before pouring herself a tall glass of iced tea. She leaned one hip against the counter and glanced around in puzzlement.

Lizzie's backpack wasn't hanging on the hook behind the door, as it should be at—Grace checked her watch—almost four o'clock. A faint stirring of worry fluttered in the depth of her brain, but she pushed it away. Jack had promised.

Besides, the door had been left open. Which meant *someone* had been here.

She checked her phone for a message. Nothing. She scanned the room for a note he might have left to explain, but found none. But why would there be? Jack couldn't climb the stairs!

Had Lizzie even arrived home? Grace dialed the school but got only an automated response. Worry took a tighter stranglehold.

Why aren't you here, Jack? Why couldn't you keep your promise?

Grace abandoned her iced tea, grabbed her car keys and stepped outside. She walked to the main house but no one answered the door. Mandy was barrel training in her riding ring, but when Grace walked up, she rode her horse to the fence.

"Hi, Miss P. How are—oh, dear. You look upset," Mandy said. "What's wrong?"

"I can't seem to find Lizzie," Grace explained. "Jack was supposed to be here when she got home from school, but he's missing, too. Could he have forgotten and gone with the chuck wagon again?"

"Jack took over care of Lizzie when her parents died. That doesn't strike me as something an irresponsible man would do," Mandy said quietly. She stared straight at Grace. "Is that how you see him? Irresponsible?"

"No, of course not." She *had* been thinking that! Feeling ashamed of herself, Grace explained, "It's just that they should be here. And they're not so I'm worried."

"It is weird." Mandy thought for a moment. "Have you checked with Sam? Joy will be at the bakery, of course, but he usually meets the school bus here."

"Of course," Grace said hurriedly. "I'll check if Lizzie's with them. Thanks." While Mandy returned to work, she dialed Sam's number. No answer.

Worry mushroomed into an oppressive cloud that Grace couldn't shake. What if the child was in trouble? Would Lizzie know who to contact? Could she have wandered away into the woods?

Afraid, concerned and uncertain what to do next, Grace got into her car. But where to go? She turned to the one source of help that had guided her through her life.

"I don't know where to start to look for her," she prayed. "Please show me."

"Miss P.!" That familiar childish yell was music to her ears.

Grace jumped out of the car and immediately spotted Lizzie racing toward her. Her heart welled with relief as she gave thanks for the quick answer to prayer.

"Lizzie, I've been looking—" She stopped short, shocked by the tear-ravaged face. "What's wrong, dear? Is it Jack?" she asked as fear amped up.

"Pops? Uh-uh. It's Bonnie. You gotta come quick," the child pleaded. "She's hurt an' it's my fault."

"Settle down now." Grace fought to sound calm and competent, though she felt anything but. "Show me where she is."

"At the petting zoo." Lizzie raced ahead, then waited impatiently by the gate. "Come *on*," she urged.

"I'm here and—oh, dear." Grace's heart sank.

Inside the pen, Bonnie sat on the ground, leaning against the fence. There was blood smeared across her face and she was pressing the cuff of her blood-stained sleeve against her forehead.

"What happened?" Grace peeked at the wound and winced.

"It looks worse than it is," Bonnie insisted, though her face was drawn and white. "I wasn't watching my step. Cecily, that's the mama goat, nudged me. I tripped over the hoe and took a tumble right onto its sharp edge."

"'Cause I left the hoe there. I was s'posed to put it away an' I dint," Lizzie admitted with a sob. "I'm sorry, Miss Bonnie. Pops is gonna be real mad at me."

"No, he's not because it wasn't your fault," Bonnie reassured her.

"But speaking of Jack," Grace interjected. "Where is he? Anyone know?"

"He and Ben went out this morning." Bonnie frowned. "Back into the hills. I was baking pies or I would have gone along. Ben said Jack was going with him and promised me they'd return before lunch. When they didn't show up, I sent Oliver to check on them, but he's not back yet either."

"Well, *Pops* and I will have a discussion later," Grace promised grimly. "But right now, we need to get you to the hospital, Bonnie. This cut needs stitches."

"I'm fine—"

"You're not, dear. But you will be. Can you stand?" She supported Bonnie as she struggled to her feet and when she wavered a bit, Grace held steady, soothing in her calmest voice, "Easy now.

We'll slowly walk over to that bench by the big cottonwood tree. Can you make it?"

"Of course." Bonnie forced a smile, but once she reached the bench, she sank onto it with obvious relief.

"Good job," Grace praised, knowing her hostess must be in some pain to allow that grimace. "You two stay here while I get my car."

After cleaning and stitching the wound, the medical staff at the hospital wanted to keep Bonnie for a few hours to be certain everything was all right. Grace was prepared to wait but Bonnie insisted she return to the ranch.

"The rodeo meeting was supposed to start ten minutes ago," Bonnie reminded her. "They'll all be waiting. Can you make coffee and serve the pies I baked this morning?"

"Of course. Don't worry about a thing. Just rest and feel better." Reassured her friend would be well cared for, Grace and Lizzie drove back to the ranch.

Though her irritation with Jack had faded in light of Bonnie's emergency, it reignited when she found Ben and Jack in the main house, calmly hosting the rodeo meeting at the dining room table. She frowned at the tall glasses of iced tea sitting on the bare table while droplets condensed on the lovely wood as the group laughed, joked and ate Bonnie's pie.

Grace called Ben aside and explained about

his wife's accident. The rancher immediately excused himself and hurried away, his concern obvious. Grace cleared her throat and interrupted the discussion.

"Can we break for a minute to get coasters and napkins?" she asked pleasantly. "I'd sure hate for us to mark up this hundred-year-old table."

Once protection was in place to preserve Bonnie's family treasure, Grace poured iced tea for herself and Lizzie. Then they sat in the chairs someone had thoughtfully brought from the kitchen.

"I'm sorry we're late," she said, annoyed that Jack looked so unconcerned. Had he forgotten he was to meet Lizzie? "Our delay was unavoidable. Now what have you done so far?"

"Is Lizzie staying?" Jack asked, one eyebrow arched.

"Of course." Did he think Grace intended to miss another meeting? "Unless you have someone to be with her, she's going to sit here and draw some pictures." After tearing two sheets out of her notebook and handing the child a pen, she gave him a wide-eyed stare. "I'm sorry. Had you planned something else for *after* you met her bus?"

"I don't have anything but this meeting planned," he said evenly, holding her gaze.

Was he going to pretend he'd met the bus? Her temper began to simmer.

"Okay, folks. Let's get started," he said with a jovial smile for the others. "I have some rodeo ideas I want to share with you."

"Oh. So do I." Grace smiled at the group, hoping to cut the tension that hung in the room. Everyone was looking from her to Jack, as if they knew something was brewing between them. Well, she wouldn't give them the satisfaction. "Let's get planning."

She made notes each time a consensus was reached, surprised by how easily Jack took over as chair of the group. He had a natural ability at making people feel comfortable.

"Next, let's talk about advertising." Jack laid out some of his photos. "I thought we could use some of these, if you agree?" Nods of approval. "Any preference?" The group selected several for the brochure, which he volunteered to put together and have printed.

Agreeing on the actual events to be held took much longer, but eventually an outline of the rodeo began to take shape.

"Sounds like we've got things well under control," Jack said. "We've nailed down most everything. So if there's nothing else, we'll adjourn."

When no one spoke, Grace frowned. Jack had said he had experience at holding rodeos. So...?

"I have a few questions." All heads turned toward her. "What if it rains that weekend? Or if it's baking hot? And what about bathroom facilities? We can't have people tramping in and out of this house. That wouldn't be fair to Bonnie or Ben." She went on listing the need for food and drinks, for activities for smaller children.

"This is a rodeo, Grace," Jack interrupted. "For kids who *ride*."

"Yes, but the riders aren't going to come by themselves." Irritated that he sounded condescending, she elaborated. "What parent will leave behind their younger children to come? We should have something for those children to do. Perhaps we could rent a bouncy castle? Or maybe a trampoline? Put up some tire swings?"

"That's not going to raise money for us," someone said.

"It might pay off if we hold the event again next year. Word will get out that families are welcome," Grace replied calmly. "There also might be an opportunity to grow our rodeo by adding events for the younger kids."

"I like that idea," one of the group members agreed. "That would bring us some funds every year for a big project at the camp. There's always something needs doing there."

"Not everyone will bring a picnic lunch, even if we ask them to," another one called. "What about food, Grace?"

"There must be a food truck we could hire," Jack said. "Or maybe we could pay one of the local eateries to supply it?"

"No," Grace said firmly.

"Why not?" Jack stared at her, his forehead pleated. "That's what we did in Texas."

"I'm sure it worked well for you," she said agreeably. "But this is a fund-raiser." He nodded and she continued. "We don't want to give away money the camp badly needs to a food truck from out of town. Also…" She paused, nervously aware that everyone was staring at her. She hesitated and scanned the room, suddenly unsure of herself.

Sometime during the proceedings, the Calhoun brothers had come in. They'd stood in the doorway, listening. Grace glanced at Sam, who smiled.

"Go on, Miss P.," Sam said. "Tell us your ideas."

"Well." She inhaled. "There may be some folks who come to the rodeo because they associate the Double H with Sunshine and the Experience Christmas events that we held last December. They'll expect a full-service experience, just like they did then."

"It's just a rodeo, Grace," Jack said impatiently.

"For now. But if we plan properly, it could turn into the camp's yearly major fund-raiser." She glanced around the table. "Also, I doubt we want to go to all the work of drawing people here and then sending them away to get something to eat and drink."

"Good point," someone said with a nod.

"Thank you." She continued. "This is a rodeo. We should provide rodeo food. Chili, hamburgers, lemonade, pies—"

"But, Gracie," Jack interrupted. "Who's going to prepare, cook and serve all that?"

"The Sunshine Ladies' Group," she announced. "This could be an all-inclusive project, Jack, with everyone who wants to playing a part. Besides." She deliberately waited for complete silence before continuing. "With the money the ladies' group raises from food sales, they may be able to begin a fund for pool repairs at camp. It desperately needs some work, too."

She fidgeted in her chair, uncomfortable now with the prolonged silence and the way everyone was staring at her. No one spoke. Maybe she should have let Jack adjourn.

Had she gone too far?

"I like it," Jack said suddenly. "Big plans and big expectations. Let's go for it."

Smiles, laughter—the tension dissipated as ideas poured out.

"If we get as many entrants as Grace is talking about, we will need bathrooms." Jeff Anderson nodded. "I'll handle that area."

"Frank, you're the insurance agent. Can you find out what we'll need for coverage in case someone is hurt?" Jack asked. "Gracie, you're noting all this, right?"

She nodded and kept writing until Drew cleared his throat.

"Since this rodeo is on the family ranch, we want to be part of it, too." Drew looked at his brothers. "We'll volunteer to set up an area in our Peace Meadow with lots of activities for the younger ones. Maybe we can find sitters to free the parents so they can watch their participants. It will also make the rodeo safer by keeping the little kids busy and away from the horses."

Sam and Zac volunteered to help.

"What else needs doing, Gracie?" Somehow, she didn't mind Jack calling her that now. Strange.

She suggested more areas of concern and the brothers chose those they could handle, leaving the rest to volunteers.

"That's all I have noted for the moment," she told the group when everything was checked off. "Whatever else we come up with, we'll discuss at the next meeting."

"Miss P., you are a genius. It's clear you've put a lot of thought into the details of holding this rodeo." Sam grinned as he bent over and hugged her.

"Why not have Grace cochair the lead on the rodeo committee?"

"Oh, no," she demurred, suspecting Jack wanted that position. "Ben's doing a fine job. I'm just here to help."

"Miss P. helps everybody," Lizzie said. "That's

what you said. Isn't it, Pops?" She peered at her grandfather.

"I sure did, Sweet Pea. Gracie's a born organizer." The gracious and fulsome praise from Jack was totally unexpected. So was his wink. Gracie gulped as her heart rate ramped up. "Fact is, your ladies' group has already begun planning ways to help with the rodeo, including the menu. Am I right?"

"Well, yes," she admitted, unable to do anything about the color flooding her face because of his appreciative stare.

"So, all we have to do is follow Miss P.'s directions," Drew joked. Everyone laughed.

Grace appreciated this confidence in her, but with Jess's place to take care of, with Lizzie and with filling in for Jack, she didn't really want even more responsibility. She also didn't have a lot of knowledge about rodeos.

She was about to decline when she noticed Jack's face. His narrowed gaze was on her and he was frowning. Because he didn't think she could handle the job? Because she was only good for libraries and looking after Lizzie? Grace mentally bristled.

Jack talked a good game. He pretended he trusted her and believed in her. He said all the right words. But was the truth that he actually had no faith in her? Was that why he wanted to marry her, so he could be in control of things? A thousand doubts filled her head until everything whirled together and she couldn't separate feeling from truth.

But Grace knew one thing for sure. She had always had a soft spot for Jack Prinz. He made her feel things, dream things that she'd never before imagined. At his best, Jack was funny and sweet and brought joy to her world. In spite of her denials, the crush she'd had at fifteen had now matured and bloomed and deepened into something that, if not love, was as close to it as she'd ever been.

But she *could not* marry Jack. She *would not* marry a man who didn't believe in her, who wouldn't be there to give her his total confidence and full support, who wouldn't cheer her on. But that wasn't the only reason why marriage was impossible.

Today had brought Grace new perspective and with it, self-realization and the disquieting knowledge that though she cared a great deal about Jack, *she* didn't believe in *him* either, not completely.

Not as a *wife* should.

"I'm afraid I couldn't possibly be cochair," she blurted and turned to Jack. "You and Ben know way more about rodeos than I do. I'd prefer to stay in the background on this, though I'm happy to help however I can."

Maybe if she had more time to see how Jack

worked with the committee, she could figure out if she truly *wanted* to build a closer relationship with him. And perhaps, with time, Jack would begin to see her as more than just a librarian who was good with Lizzie.

At least I hope that's where You're leading me.

Something was off with Gracie.

Jack sensed it the moment she refused to accept the position of rodeo cochair. It wasn't the way she declined, not because of a tremor in her voice or anything like that. It wasn't even that she'd said she preferred the background, as if she could ever be in the background, unnoticed.

As soon as the meeting was adjourned, she'd excused herself, taken Lizzie and left. For the past two days she'd shuttered herself inside the log house, sending Lizzie out with his meals.

Then, last night, on the verge of sleep, Jack had suddenly remembered the way Gracie had looked at him at the end of the meeting. She'd gazed across Bonnie and Ben's table, violet eyes dulled, erect shoulders slumped, as if she'd lost every special feature that made her who she was. Right after Drew had made his joke, that's when something had changed, something important, something he was pretty sure he couldn't make better with all the sweet talk in the world.

Something that meant Gracie Partridge was testing him.

But why and about what?

He was pretty sure the why had to do with his failure to meet Lizzie's bus that day. So it was time to make amends.

Jack ambled across the yard and tossed some gravel at the door. The bus had come and gone with Lizzie. Grace would be alone now. They could talk.

He hoped.

The door opened, but she didn't look at him. She was on the phone.

"I'm sure you'll find a way, Jess. You've talked about riding a camel for eons. You can make this happen. Talk to the shore excursions person on the ship. They'll have a way to arrange it if you really want to go." Finally she lifted her head.

Jack pointed to the picnic table. She nodded but continued her conversation.

"I'm so glad you're enjoying it," she said, though there was nothing in her expression that spoke of gladness. "No, nothing new here, but I do have to go now. I'll talk to you again soon, okay? Bye."

She tucked her phone in her pocket, grabbed an insulated mug and joined him at the table. "Do you need something more for breakfast?"

"No. Thank you." Maybe this wasn't the right time, but—"Have you got a minute to talk, Grace?" Jack asked.

"I suppose. But I need a comfier chair than

those benches." She chose one of the big Adirondack chairs and sank into it. Jack sat next to her.

"I'm sorry about the other day and not meeting the bus," he began. "Lizzie told me you were worried. I never meant to cause you that."

"You never do." It was not an accusation. It was said in a flat tone of acceptance.

Which he hated. Because it was important that she think better of him?

"We should have been back well before Lizzie came home. But we broke something on the vehicle and there was no cell reception in that valley."

"Uh-huh. Bonnie told me she noticed no one had met Lizzie so she stepped in. Thankfully." She sipped her coffee, her gaze fixed on something to the left of him, though Jack saw nothing that would require such attention.

"I'm trying to apologize, Gracie."

"My name is Grace." She studied him, her attitude distant. "Apologize for what?"

"For not being here when Lizzie got home." He should have said more, but he wasn't sure that was what she wanted to hear from him. "For worrying you."

"You already said it wasn't your fault. Anyway, *I* wasn't that worried," Gracie told him, again in that chilly voice that was so unlike her warm personality. "But Lizzie would have been. Wouldn't you be if you were a five-year-old child with no one to meet you when you got off the school bus?"

"Almost six," he joked. Gracie was not amused.

"If Bonnie hadn't been here, hadn't realized that no one was home for Lizzie, that she was all alone over here…" She let it trail away. "Don't you feel any responsibility for her?" she asked after some time had passed and she couldn't repress her annoyance any longer. "Do you care so little for your own granddaughter that you'll dump her on the first willing person who comes along so you can have your freedom—to take *pictures*?"

"I was trying to get good shots for the rodeo brochure," he argued as irritation flared. What was behind this inquisition?

"You already *had* good shots, Jack. Many of them," she added. "In fact, I was under the impression that we'd already chosen several, the very ones you showed to the rodeo group that afternoon." Grace looked straight at him, waiting. For what?

"I want everything to be first quality," he bristled.

"If you keep on reaching for perfection, you're going to seriously and negatively impact our rodeo. Those pamphlets should have been printed immediately after the meeting. And yet you went out to take even more shots yesterday. Why?"

"I was trying—" He faltered, unable to come

up with a solid excuse and uncomfortable under her stare.

"Trying to do what?" Grace kept hammering. "Don't you want to spend time with your granddaughter? Are you afraid of her, Jack?"

"Of course I'm not afraid of her! I love Lizzie," he snapped in exasperation and then wondered if love was the right word. Maybe he only thought he loved her. Maybe he was as incapable of love as he was unlovable.

"So you love her. Just not enough to spend time with her." She shook her head when he blustered for a response and continued. "You've missed five consecutive evening story times with her, Jack."

"I had—"

"Something more important to do?" Her eyebrow arched. "She's a little girl who should be dreaming of fairy tales. Yet she lies awake, wondering why her pops didn't kiss her good-night, didn't tell her that he loves her." Grace leaned forward, locked gazes with him. "And you never came. You never said what she longed to hear so she could fall asleep secure in the knowledge that the person she loves the most feels the same about her."

Jack had nothing with which to defend himself so he remained silent, hugging his secret to himself.

"You're doing to her what your father did to you."

"Never," he said with loathing.

"Then explain why you're avoiding spending time with her. Lately you dump Lizzie on me, or Bonnie, the Calhoun wives or whoever is convenient at the moment. You divest yourself of responsibility as often as you can and I need to understand why."

"I do love Lizzie," Jack muttered. He lifted his head and stared at her. "I'm just not like you, Gracie."

"Like me?" She drew back in dismay. "What does that mean?"

"You take on everything without fear," he said quietly. "You know what's right and you don't back down at a challenge."

"Neither do you," she said immediately. Then she frowned and added, "Do you?"

"Sometimes. I'm useless when it comes to feelings."

"I don't understand how that relates—"

"Just listen for a minute." Trapped, Jack raked a hand through his hair and wondered if what he was about to say would sound stupid. "I've heard a lot about you and your part in that Experience Christmas thing you did. Sam says you helped pull together the entire community for that event. You inspire people, Gracie."

"I don't think so." She wrinkled her nose and shook her head. "I just try to help, but sometimes I try too hard, and—I told you. Folks get offended." She sounded chastened by her own admission.

"Probably because they don't understand, at least not right away," he said quietly.

"Understand what?"

"That your sole goal is to help. Help people. Help your friend Jess. Help the town. Help make the world better." Jack smiled at her. "That's who you are."

"That's silly," she said, her cheeks turning a bright pink. "I'm just Sunshine's former librarian."

"If that's what I thought when I first came here, it isn't true now. You are much more than that, Grace," Jack told her and meant it. "I admire you far beyond what I can articulate. I'm sorry if you feel that I've underestimated you." He watched her deal with his words and winced as suspicion filled her lovely face. He'd hurt her without meaning to.

"You're doing it again." Her jaw tensed and her chin lifted.

"Doing what?"

"Playing games. Trying to flatter me, to get me charmed and confused so I'll forget my point and then you'll be able to walk away without facing the truth."

"I am not trying to do that, but what is your point?" He waited, surprised that she easily recognized and was willing to call him out on the behavior he so often resorted to. "Come on, explain," he encouraged. "You help everyone else. You can try to help me, can't you?"

He'd half meant it as a joke, but as he said it, he knew he truly wanted her help. Grace didn't back down.

"The thing is," she began slowly, as if searching her way through a maze. "I think you have to *want* to be helped, Jack, and I'm not sure you do. I think you've become comfortable with this game of self-sufficiency you play. But I don't play games, Jack. I don't know how."

"I'm not playing games," he promised, not exactly sure why he wanted her help, but certain he needed it. He'd followed his own path for so long, kept his loneliness and pain hidden, pretended everything was fine. Only it wasn't. He knew it.

And Grace knew it, too.

"This might hurt you to hear," she murmured, her voice gentle.

"Say it anyway." He shrugged and grinned. "I'm a tough cowboy, remember?"

"Very well." She exhaled but held his gaze like a laser beam. "When you ran away from home… I think you were trying to protect yourself. You loved your father, but he couldn't or wouldn't show you love, so the only way to make it hurt less was for you to run away."

"True, and it was a good move. I ended up with

Milt," he told her, trying to infuse some lightness into the memories.

"Did you love Milt?"

Grace's question rocked Jack. He frowned, struggling to find an answer.

"No games, remember?"

"I cared for him a great deal," he said slowly. "I guess some people would say I loved him."

"But you wouldn't say that?" she pressed.

"I don't have much use for the word *love*," he admitted. "We love pie. We love coffee. People say it so often it's become meaningless."

"It's not just saying the word though, is it?" She studied him so intently he wanted to turn away. Yet he couldn't. "You don't want to *feel* love because it hurts if it's not reciprocated. Like it hurt with your father. That's why you won't let anyone get too close, including sweet little Lizzie," she added very softly. "Because she might hurt you."

"I care about Lizzie more than anything in this world."

"Yes, but you didn't say love. Because you can't." Grace said it as if a light had gone on. "That's why you said that if we marry, you won't love me. Because love threatens you. But Lizzie loves you and needs you to love her…" She paused to let her words sink in. "You want to marry me, Jack, but not because you care for me. You're angling for marriage so you won't be vulnerable to hurt, but you'll still be certain Lizzie's taken care of. Because I do love her."

Jack said nothing. What could he say? She was too close to the truth.

Grace remained silent for a long time, obviously sorting things through in her mind. Jack kept quiet because he didn't want to reveal anything else. Looking weak—he'd avoided that all these years. He wasn't about to bare his soul now.

"Actually, Jack, the problem is you *do* love Lizzie." Grace sighed. "But you're desperately afraid of that love. You don't trust it, just like you don't trust me."

"What?" Jack stared at her. "I trust you. I wouldn't have asked you to marry me if I didn't."

"Your proposal had nothing to do with trust. You wanted *an agreement*, remember?" Grace smiled sadly and shook her head. "You didn't know me, don't know me even now. And I don't really know you either." Her forced smile hurt to see. "How could two strangers like us ever survive a marriage, Jack?"

He knew then that she was going to turn him down, for good. He couldn't let that happen. She was his last hope for his granddaughter. Lizzie deserved Grace in her life, to be loved and cared for by her. His granddaughter deserved to have this woman give her all the things he didn't know she needed, let alone know how to give them.

Jack had to make that happen, no matter what it cost him.

"You want to really know me, Gracie? You think knowing my past will make a marriage between us work?" Jack said, angry and yet somehow relieved that she'd pushed him into this corner. "Then buckle up, lady, because you're about to hear the whole truth about me and it sure isn't pretty."

Chapter Ten

Grace wasn't exactly sure what she'd unleashed, but it was too late to stop Jack now, even if she wanted to.

Which she didn't.

What she wanted, no needed, was to understand what had driven this man to completely eschew love. If only to soften the pain of knowing that he wasn't the answer to a prayer she'd prayed her whole life.

"I'm listening, Jack."

"I told you about Milt taking me in," he began, his finger thrumming against the picnic table as if the words waited to escape. "He was a great guy, but he wasn't well. By the time I arrived at the ranch he'd already weathered two cancer scares." He shook his head at her questioning stare. "I didn't know about them until one day when I was twenty-two and he suddenly passed out. I took him to the hospital. They said the cancer was back, this time in his lungs."

"Oh no." Grace gasped with dismay.

"It wasn't a good situation. Milt went through surgery and treatment. He survived it and for some time he seemed to be doing well. But he was growing frailer." Jack stared at his hands. "I worked myself crazy to keep the ranch going so he wouldn't feel compelled to help on days when he felt bad." Jack looked straight at her. "I did everything I could to ease his mind and spirit. Including, eventually, proposing to Sheena."

"What?" Had she heard that right? "Wait! I need another cup of coffee." Grace jumped to her feet. "Do you want one, too?"

"Sure." Jack gave her an odd smile. "Now who's running, Gracie?"

"I'm not. I'll be right back." She rushed up the stairs and into the log house as if chased. While the coffee dripped, she reviewed what he'd said. Jack had proposed to Sheena for Milt's sake?

Meaning he'd never loved his wife?

Confused and concerned about what she'd hear next, Grace quickly poured the brew into the two insulated mugs, added cream to her own and carried both outside. The day was warming thanks to a brilliant sun, but it wasn't hot and there were no rain clouds in sight so inclement weather wouldn't be her excuse to escape again, if she needed it.

Lord, help me hear this without judging Jack. Please give me the right words to say to support him.

After a sip of coffee, she smiled at him.

"That's better. Sorry for the interruption. Please continue."

"You don't want to hear this." Jack stared at his mug. "Too much information, and all that."

"I want to hear anything you want to tell me," she assured him. "Please, go on."

"Sheena was Milt's niece," he said quietly. "I knew her for a couple of years, enough to say hello, but not much more than that. She ran an eatery place in town and she sure could cook." He stared into the distance. "She used to come to the ranch now and then to bring Milt a treat. He devoured it, though he never ate much of what I prepared."

"Oh." Grace realized she was holding her breath and expelled it.

"Anyway, one day when Sheena stopped by, Milt asked me to take her riding because she hadn't been able to ride since her parents had sold their ranch and moved away. I did." He shrugged. "Later that night Milt talked a lot about her, how she knew all about ranching. He suggested I consider asking her to marry me, that she'd be a good ranch wife and he wouldn't mind eating her cooking every day."

"That's why you married her?" Grace was aghast.

"Sort of." Jack licked his lips. "You have to understand that from the day I moved in, Milt was always worrying about me. He admitted that as his illness progressed, he'd been fussing over what would happen to me when he died. He desperately wanted an heir for his ranch."

"An heir?" She gasped.

"Someone who would carry on his ranch, he meant." Jack frowned. "It sounds stupid now, but he was old and ill and my best friend. I couldn't refuse him anything. He kept after me, telling me all about Sheena's great characteristics until I finally took her out a couple of times, just to please him. He loved that. He wanted her to spend Christmas with us that year, to have a big Christmas dinner with all the fixings."

"You agreed."

"Yes, for Milt. He'd been fighting his disease for several years by then so he was pretty weak. He ate like a bird. I was worried he didn't have much time left and I figured that if her being there made his last days happy, it was worth it."

"That was kind of you," she murmured.

"It was a good Christmas," he said, his voice soft, full of memories. "Milt laughed and joked like in the old days. After Sheena went home, I gave him his gift. He thanked me. Then, very quietly, he said the best gift I could ever give him was to settle down with Sheena and have a family. Then he could rest easy."

Grace remained silent. What was there to say?

"I never loved Sheena," he said finally, after a long pause. "But I liked her. She was great with Milt." The words stopped, then restarted in a rush. "And I wanted a family like other people had. I wanted someone to care about, who would care about me. Milt was all I had by then and I believed he could die at any time. I think I was afraid to be alone."

"Did you pray about marrying Sheena?" Grace murmured, greatly moved by his heartrending explanation.

"I didn't pray about anything in those days." Jack's face wore a faraway look. "Except for God to make Milt better. He didn't."

"But—" Grace obeyed an inner voice that whispered, *Wait.*

"Anyway, Milt kept pressing and Sheena seemed to enjoy herself when we were together, so I finally asked her to marry me and she agreed. She seemed very happy, talking all the time about wedding plans. Milt rallied at the news. He insisted we had to do it right so I went along with whatever they wanted. I was really busy then anyway but I never expected a town-wide event. A show." His mouth turned down.

Grace didn't know what to say so she slid her hand into his and squeezed. He glanced at her hand but didn't let go as he continued his story in a flat, lifeless tone.

"A week after we were married, Sheena told me she'd sold her café. No discussion, no asking my opinion, no sharing, nothing. Done deed." He shrugged. "It was her business and none of mine so I kept quiet. Anyway, she said she needed to be on the ranch full-time to care for Milt. I liked that. But then I started coming home and finding out she'd been gone all day. She never said where. I didn't think I needed to ask."

Oh no. Grace held her breath in anticipation of the worst.

"Anyway, Sheena got pregnant right away and then Cade arrived. With his birth, everything changed. She changed."

"How?" Grace asked softly, drawing her hand away because his touch made her wish she'd known him then, could have done something to help. There was such an aura of sadness in his words and in the way his proud shoulders seemed to droop and sink. If only...

"Sheena insisted the house needed immediate redoing, that it was outdated, an embarrassment." He bit his lip. "It wasn't true. Milt was big on up-keep, but maybe it wasn't her style. I told her I couldn't afford it. Then one day I overheard her begging him to pay for a total gut job. She said she wouldn't stay unless it happened."

"Wouldn't stay?" Fear clogged Grace's throat.

"As in she would leave. With Cade." Jack combed his hand through his hair, his face white. "Milt, weakened and needing peace in his world, immediately agreed to the renovation."

"Poor man," she whispered.

"I couldn't understand her. I thought we had a solid marriage. We had a son."

The world around them fell silent, waiting. Grace held her breath.

"Sheena had said she loved me and I believed

her, you see. Because nobody ever said that to me before," he murmured. He lifted his head and stared at her. "Except for you, Gracie."

When he didn't immediately continue, Grace knew the story would go downhill from here. She began silently praying.

"I was so hurt that I called her out on bugging Milt when he wasn't well." Pain welled in his forlorn eyes.

"Oh, Jack." Her heart broke for his disillusionment. "Don't tell me if you don't want to," she murmured. "Some things are just too private—"

"Private?" he scoffed, his face tight with anger and pain. "Her affair wasn't private. A friend told me after the renovation was complete that Sheena had been seeing her old boyfriend since before we'd been married, long before Cade's birth. When I confronted her, she laughed, said she'd never loved me. She'd only said that so I would marry her. Because the boyfriend wouldn't."

"You don't have to say any more," Grace told him, her heart breaking for this proud man's suffering.

"You should hear it all." He licked his lips and then sipped his coffee. Finally, he continued. "She said Cade wasn't mine and that I would never be his father."

Aghast, Grace tightened her hold on his hand. *Lord, please help me help him.*

"It got nasty then with all kinds of terrible things

said. Sheena refused to divorce. When I pressed the issue, she threatened to spread vicious rumors of abuse. She threatened to tell them to Milt so he would cut me out of his will. I didn't care about the will, but I couldn't allow anything to hurt that very kind man, so I stopped fighting her."

"That must have truly tested you, Jack." Such an inadequate response.

"Yeah." A horrible smile curled his lips. "But at least I finally understood that our marriage was all about the money, Milt's money, of which she would get half after his death. I understood that all Sheena wanted from me was the prestige of being a wealthy rancher's wife and a solid bank account. She wouldn't divorce because she wanted to flaunt our wealth and status, to make the boyfriend jealous even more because he was getting married. To someone else." Jack's lips curled cruelly.

Oh, Lord, Grace prayed the phrase repeatedly, soundlessly.

"Eventually I had a paternity test done, without her knowledge. Cade wasn't my biological son, but he *was* my son in name at least. Sheena ran me down to Cade every chance she got, but I hung in those years because I cared about him and because I wanted him to know Milt. And he did. They developed a very strong bond even though Milt grew increasingly more ill. I think Cade was the reason why he kept hanging on."

"I'm glad he did," Grace said, brushing away her tears.

"Me, too." Jack managed a smile. "Then, just after Cade turned ten, Sheena found out she had a very aggressive cancer. She and Milt passed away within two weeks of each other," he said very quietly. "It was as if he was waiting for her to leave first, as if he wanted to make sure we'd be okay."

Jack stopped, closed his eyes and exhaled as if shedding the world from his shoulders.

"I am so sorry," Grace said, thinking how weak that sounded.

"Don't be. That's when I knew for sure that I was no good at love, that I wasn't lovable, as my father had said." The words came so quietly she almost didn't hear. "If my wife and my own father couldn't love me, the problem must be me."

"And Cade?" She was half-afraid to hear the answer.

"Cade and I came to terms with things," Jack said quietly. "I never said anything against Sheena. She was his mother. But I think that as he grew older, he understood. He adored Milt and wanted to carry on his ranch. I was good with that."

"Because you wanted to indulge your love of photography." She smiled at his questioning look. "Lizzie told me about you coming and going from the ranch."

"I couldn't stay there," he said bluntly. "All the

good times I'd had with Milt were colored by— I just couldn't stay."

Grace leaned back in her chair, letting the sun warm her face, absorbing what he'd told her into her mental picture of this man's character. So much loss it made her want to weep.

"Where do we go from here, Gracie?" Jack touched her arm as if to rouse her. "This ranch, Sunshine—it's a good place to make a fresh start."

And suddenly she was thrust into the past, to the day before he'd left town, when they'd gone for a walk and sat in the high grass, sharing one final goodbye.

Know what, Gracie? When you have that family you're always talking about, make sure they know you love them. Tell them over and over until they ask you to stop saying it. And then tell them again. That's what I wish my dad would do.

"You're a wonderful woman, Grace. You understand all the ins and outs about loving and caring. I was blessed to know you back then, and Lizzie and I are blessed now." His hand slid up to her cheek and he cupped his palm around it, his dark gaze meeting hers. "You're the perfect grandmother for Lizzie because you will always go to bat on her behalf. Like you did today, against me."

"Well, you *were* shirking your duty," she murmured in self-defense.

Jack burst out laughing.

"I was," he agreed. "I won't do it again. But

what about marrying me? Now that you know my horrible secrets, is marriage still out of the question?"

How could she say she was still waiting on leading from God?

"I will never find anyone more perfect for Sweet Pea," he said as his hand dropped away. "And I think we need to decide soon."

"You've already decided." Grace knew it was true.

"Yes, I have. And nothing that's happened since we came to the Double H has changed my mind." He smiled and this time there was no pretense or acting there. She felt he was speaking from the heart. "I think you'd make a wonderful wife and you've already proven yourself with Lizzie. The question is, can you tolerate the idea of being married to me, knowing how badly I failed at marriage?"

"You didn't fail," she insisted staunchly. "But it's not that."

"Then...?" Jack leaned back into his chair, frowning as he shifted his leg to a more comfortable position. "If I spend forever searching, I'd never find anyone as perfect for my granddaughter or for me as you." He paused. "But living as we are—it's an artificial situation that can't last. I want, I *need* something more permanent."

"Marriage is certainly that," she agreed.

"It's going to totally disrupt Lizzie's life if I

have to tell her we can't stay with you," he said coaxingly. "She loves you, Grace. She leans on and confides in you. She turns to you for comfort. You two are getting very close."

"She's a delightful child and I love her very much." Grace met his gaze head-on and voiced the one word that kept filling her mind. "But."

"I'm sorry if you think I'm rushing you, Gracie. It's not my intent. But I need to get my future settled."

"What are you saying, Jack?" She frowned, not liking the sound of this.

"I'm saying that I will stay here on the ranch, until the rodeo is over. I promised to help with that and I will." His voice came strong now, firm. "But then, when I'm fully recovered, I'm going to ask you one last time. If you feel you can't marry me, then I won't like it but Lizzie and I will leave."

Stunned by his ultimatum, Grace couldn't find anything to say as he rose, settled his crutches and walked away.

God? What am I supposed to do?

She waited for a very long time. But there was no response.

"I hope you don't mind me stopping by." Jack stood in the doorway of Pastor Ed's office as questions about what he was doing here raced through his head.

"Come in, Jack. I've got my coffee maker all ready." The man waved him to a comfy chair and took the one opposite. "I'm glad you called. I've been wanting to call you but wasn't sure you wanted to hear from me."

"I guess I haven't exactly been cordial these last three visits to your church," Jack admitted. "I only came because Gracie and Lizzie were coming."

"Doesn't matter why you came. You're always welcome." Pastor Ed gave him a sunny smile. "What would you like to drink?"

"I'm kind of partial to iced coffee." When he had the beverage in hand and Ed was seated once more, he didn't know where to start. Finally, he blurted it out. "How do you make someone love you?"

To his credit, Ed took it in stride.

"I'm not sure anyone can *make* someone love them. Love is a gift from God." Ed sipped his own coffee for a few minutes. "Why don't you tell me what's really bugging you, Jack?"

Jack had struggled with this for two weeks since his talk with Gracie. And he was sick of it. If there was a way that he could know that God truly loved him, that he wasn't the misfit he'd always felt, he needed to find it.

Then maybe, just maybe, he could become the kind of man Grace would want to marry.

"I'm a preacher's kid," he said. "I heard my father talk a lot about God's love. But I never saw or felt loved by him, and especially not by God."

"That doesn't mean God doesn't love you, Jack," Ed countered. "Or that your dad didn't. It just means that we humans often fail to reflect His love. I'm afraid humans fail that way a lot. Including me."

"You're saying God loves me?" Same old, same old. Maybe he shouldn't have expected the minister to help.

"It's not just me who's saying it, Jack. In First John, the Bible says, *God is love.* Which means God can't help loving you, because He *is* love. Always. No matter what."

"I'm not sure I understand that." Jack frowned.

"Join the club. I doubt anyone fully understands God's love, any more than we can understand human love. The difference," Ed said with a grin, "is that God's love doesn't end. Can I ask you something?"

"I guess." Why did he suddenly feel he needed to be on guard?

"Why do you come to church with Grace if you don't believe in God's love?" Ed appeared relaxed as he leaned back. "I know you said it was because Grace was coming, but I have this feeling that there's another reason."

"I wanted to check out something."

Ed nodded but said nothing.

"I have some bad memories of church people,"

Jack explained on a huff of expelled air. "Don't get me wrong—there were lots of really good folks. But there were also an awful lot of judgmental ones and they always seemed to be the ones talking about honor and integrity and forgiveness."

"Every church has those," Ed agreed.

"Yeah. But they were also the ones who constantly judged me, believed the worst about me. I was a rebellious kid who had issues with his father and God, and I acted out. A lot. But those sanctimonious folks continually believed the worst of me and judged me on that basis. And my father always sided with them. It was impossible to live up to all those expectations and demands. So I stopped trying."

"I'm no psychoanalyst," Ed said. "But I'm guessing that's when your questions about love took root."

"I never heard anyone talk about love much back then." Jack felt the sting of those long-ago judgments as strongly as ever. "All my father ever preached about was evil, punishment and God's retribution on me because of my mistakes. He couldn't understand that I had to live by my own moral code, that something inside me wouldn't let me pretend I felt what I didn't."

"You didn't feel God's love." Ed nodded. "I get it. You rejected everything your father preached because he wasn't perfect. And you're still blaming him."

"What?" Jack shook his head in surprised denial. "No. We reconciled years ago."

"You mean you said the words *I forgive you*?" Ed's voice held a touch of irony. "You did the right thing, the thing you're supposed to do. You did it after a lot of time had passed, because somebody said you needed to forgive, and, I'm just guessing here, but maybe your dad wasn't well?"

"Yes. How did you know?" Perplexed, he studied the minister.

"Doesn't matter," Ed said with a wave of his hand. "What does matter is that for you, those issues did not resolve just because you said those words. Did they?" He smiled at Jack's confusion. "Did you hear yourself a moment ago? Did you hear the bitterness in your voice when you spoke of your father? The anger, the hurt, the pain, they are all still there, locked inside of you."

Jack frowned. Was Ed right?

You're not much of a preacher's son. Why aren't you more like your sisters?

You keep making the same mistakes, Jack, because your heart is evil.

I don't have time to play games with you. I'm doing the Lord's work.

He could still hear his father's voice saying those things, still felt the hurt of them as clearly as when he was ten, twelve, eighteen. As if he'd just messed up again. The damning impact of those words *was* lodged in his head and his heart. The pain stung as it always had, gnawing at his self-esteem, sapping his joy and repeating the same song in his head, even after so many years.

"My father made me realize I was unlovable." The words emerged involuntarily.

"You still believe it, don't you? But it's a lie." Ed leaned forward. His expression grew intense as he spoke. "You are God's child, made in His image. And God is love. He loves you. And He's given you the capacity to love."

"But—"

"No buts here, Jack." Ed smiled. "Grace told me you were a rancher. So, let me ask you. If you had a system for ranching and it didn't work, would you keep using it? I doubt it. I think you're too smart for that. I think you'd say, *This system isn't working. I need a new system.* And you'd find one that did work."

"You're saying I'm stuck using an old system?"

"I'm saying you're trying to make a faulty belief, an unworkable system, work. Not gonna happen, Jack, because you started with a defective base. You started with what you *believed* your father was saying, that you're unlovable."

"That is what he meant," he said defensively.

"Could be, but it really doesn't matter what he meant. God loves you. Therefore, you *are* lovable," Ed insisted. "You must get rid of your issues with your dad and what he said. Let it all go. Otherwise it will eat you up."

"How do I do that?" Jack demanded, slightly frustrated by the simplistic-sounding response.

"I don't have any easy answers. All I can tell you is what has worked for me and some others I've counseled." Ed tilted his head as if asking whether Jack wanted to continue. At his nod, the pastor explained. "You draw a line in the sand of your mind and you say, *This ends here. I don't know why my father was the way he was and I will never know. But I forgive him for telling me this lie because God says the truth is that I am loved.*"

"That's it?" Feeling defeated, Jack wished he hadn't opened himself up for this.

"Sounds too easy, doesn't it?" Ed chuckled. "Let me tell you, brother, it is not! It is one of the hardest things you will ever do, mostly because you've held on to the lie for so long. You won't feel much at first, and you'll need to keep letting go over and over, until your heart finally obeys your head and releases the hurt."

"And then I'll be free of it?"

"Nope." Ed grinned at his blink of surprise. "Actually, you are free the moment you decide to stop believing the lies. It just takes a while to make the message sink into your head and your heart. That's where prayer and studying the Bible come in, to reaffirm God's love for you."

They talked about it for a while longer before Ed prayed for him in strong, powerful words that spoke directly to God. When he was finished, Jack raised his head and looked the pastor straight in the eye.

"Today is my line in the sand," he said clearly. "I don't know what my dad's problem was, but he was wrong. God loves me, therefore I—I am lovable," he said, faltering over the unfamiliar words.

"Again," Ed insisted and kept repeating his command until Jack was able to say it without pause, even though he didn't feel any more lovable than he had.

"Are there other things I should do that would help?" he asked.

"Read your Bible every day. It holds the truth about God. Turn to it as the only authority. Search it for answers." Ed paused, obviously hesitating over something.

"What else?" Jack asked, half-afraid to hear it.

"The Bible has two very important things to say about love. One is to love God. The other is to love your neighbor as yourself. It might help you feel lovable and loving if you begin to put loving others into practice. By showing love we become more lovable."

"I'm not sure how to do that," Jack objected.

"Pray about it. Ask God to show you. He will." Ed rose and shook his hand. "I'll be praying for you, Jack, to know how deeply and completely God loves you."

"Thank you. I can't tell you how much I appreciate this." Jack suddenly felt overwhelmed but Ed had no such inhibitions.

"Come back anytime. I'm not just a good coffee maker, you know," he joked. "Though I am very good at that."

Jack laughed all the way to the front door where he sat on a chair to wait for Ben to pick him up.

"I am lovable," he whispered to himself. "God loves me."

It felt good to say it, to plant positive messages in his mind.

And then he wondered, "Can I love?"

Gracie's lovely face floated through his mind.

A rush of vulnerability swamped him. What did he know about love? To relinquish the controls, to be at the mercy of someone else again, to open himself up to ridicule or scorn if Grace didn't love him? No!

The world turned bleak. The only thing Jack could think of was to pray. As rusty as he was, he hoped God would listen.

Chapter Eleven

There was something about Jack.

Grace didn't know what had changed in these last weeks. She knew only that this man was less bossy, less controlling and a lot less undependable than the former Jack, though he was certainly no less charismatic. And that her heart still did its crazy dance whenever he was around.

Jack was around a lot.

"You want to make cookies with us?" She stopped in the middle of the grocery-store baking aisle to stare at him, unable to believe he'd asked. "But how will you manage the steps?"

"You didn't notice." He gazed at her reproachfully before pointing to his leg. "Drew took me to the doctor yesterday and they changed my cast. My leg has healed well, but my foot still has to be secured. This boot thing makes it much easier to get around, so I should be able to handle the stairs just fine."

"Oh." She blinked, still totally nonplussed that he'd chosen to be here, with her and Lizzie, rather than taking his beloved photographs.

"Unless you don't want my help, such as it is," he added with a frown.

"Of course you should join us," she exclaimed. "Lizzie will be thrilled."

"Will you?" he said quietly, studying her face.

"I think it will be lovely if you help us bake," she temporized, not really sure how she should respond to this offer.

Yes, he certainly was different. She liked this new Jack a lot. He increasingly spent more time with them, with Lizzie of course, but also with her, instead of going off on his own. Every so often when it was just the two of them, Jack would ask questions about her faith. It was so sweet to speak to him from her heart about the God she served.

"Hey, Miss P., I got three kinds of choc'late chips," Lizzie said, tugging on her skirt to get her attention. "Is that too many?"

"Can there be too many kinds of chocolate chips?" Grace panned a shocked expression. "Let's see what you have. Chocolate, chocolate mint, and chocolate with sea salt and caramel. Delicious. Let's get home and start baking."

Two hours later they'd made three batches of cookies using all of the chocolate flavors. Jack taste tested each variety before pronouncing them all perfect.

"But why do you need so many cookies?" he asked.

Grace chuckled and pointed to the corner of her own lips to signal that he had a smear of chocolate there, but though Jack repeatedly dabbed at his mouth, he didn't remove the chocolate. She grabbed a paper towel and reached up to dab at the spot without realizing how personal that action was. Chagrined that she'd gotten so close to him, her hand froze midmotion. He grinned when she quickly stepped back, which made her wonder if he'd missed removing it on purpose.

"Thank you, Gracie," Jack murmured, his dark eyes glowing. "I'm a mess, aren't I?"

"Hardly a mess. But that apron doesn't seem to have stopped you from staining your shirt with cookie dough. But don't worry. Cookie dough doesn't diminish your debonair appearance," she teased, then caught her breath as his gaze held her motionless for a moment before she broke the connection. "Lizzie, do you want to explain what all these cookies are for?"

"Father's Day lunch tomorrow after church." Lizzie was in the midst of her own taste test.

"Brunch, but close enough." Grace laughed.

"They're so good. I hope you have enough." Jack snatched another one before she could empty the cookie sheet. "Last one, I promise."

"You've said that three times." Grace couldn't help laughing. This side of Jack, the bantering, the teasing—he was fun!

"I'll load the dishwasher and clean up. You sit down on the deck outside and enjoy your coffee," he directed.

"That's not necessary," she tried to argue but he would have none of it.

"I'm good at cleanup. Celeste taught me."

Grace glanced at the little girl, worried about how she'd react to mention of her mother. She'd tried to ease Lizzie's grief by adding phrases at the bottom of each page in Lizzie's memory books, under the pictures. Sometimes she added a scripture verse or an expression Lizzie recalled her parents using.

But because Lizzie kept asking the same questions in different ways, Grace had begun creating a whole new booklet with her own drawings, in which she posed Lizzie's questions as if a child were speaking to a teacher. She'd used her watercolors before giving it to Lizzie three days ago and was reassured that the little girl seemed to find comfort in it.

"Mommy liked things clean, didn't she, Pops?" Lizzie recalled with a giggle.

"Sparkling," Jack agreed as he filled the dishwasher with their baking utensils. "She once made me shower a second time," he said to Grace straight-faced.

"Pops!" Lizzie scolded. "That's not true."

"Well, she wanted to," he revised. "I'd been away a long time. In the desert. Celeste insisted I'd brought most of the sand home with me and was leaving it everywhere." He wiggled like a rag doll and made a comical face that had Lizzie hooting with laughter. "Go enjoy the deck now, ladies. I'm in charge here."

"Yes, sir!" Grace saluted smartly, grabbed her mug of coffee and went outside. "He's sure bossy today," she whispered loudly to Lizzie.

"I heard that," Jack called.

Grace cradled her coffee, smiling when Lizzie picked up the little book Grace had made for her and held it out.

"Can we read this?" she asked.

"Again?"

When Lizzie nodded, Grace nodded. "Sure."

"Good 'cause I like to read it. It makes me feel not so sad that I don't have a mom," the child said as she snuggled next to her. She opened to the first page and waited.

"Why don't you read it this time?" Grace smiled as she hugged the little girl closer. "You must know it by heart by now."

"All cleaned up and the dishwasher is running." Jack placed his glass of ice water on a table before sitting down. "What's that?"

"It's my own special book. See, Pops. It says Lizzie's Book right on the front." She grinned at him then at Grace. "Miss P. made it for me."

"She made you a book of your own. Wow!" Jack stared at Grace. "I didn't know you were a writer."

"I've written children's stuff for years. Christmas plays, stories, lyrics to the songs Jess dreams up. Whatever. I once hoped I'd be published, though I never got around to submitting anything. My work never seemed quite good enough." She shrugged. "I guess it's just one of those fairy-tale dreams never meant to come true." *Like getting married? Like having your own family?* She quashed the inner reminders. "Lizzie's going to read it to us now."

"My mommy and daddy went to heaven," Lizzie began. "I didn't go. Teacher said I wasn't ready. I wish I had been because then I'd be with them and I wouldn't be afraid or lonely. I could ask them all the questions I didn't get to ask before they died."

Grace made mental notes for small changes to be made here and there throughout the work, to make it flow more smoothly.

"Teacher says God is in Heaven with my mommy and daddy. He's looking after them. He must be really good at that because Teacher says they're not sad now. 'Cept that I'm not there with them. But Teacher says me being here and them being in Heaven isn't a mistake, even if it hurts a lot, 'cause God doesn't make mistakes. Not ever. But I still miss them."

As Lizzie read, Jack lifted his head and met Grace's gaze, his intense scrutiny holding her still as his granddaughter read all the things she missed about her parents. Two or three times, Lizzie's voice wobbled and she had to stop and sniff or clear her throat before turning to the next page. But for the first time since Grace had given her the book, she read straight through to the end, her voice slowing on the last few lines.

"I loved my daddy and mommy a lot. An' you know what? I'm going to see them again when I go to Heaven. Only, Teacher said that might not happen for a while. But that's okay. Know why? 'Cause Teacher says I c'n keep my mommy and daddy in my heart. Teacher says people die, but our love for them never does. Not ever. I love my mommy and daddy."

Lizzie closed the book with a little sigh.

"That was some really good reading, Sweet Pea."

Something about Jack's voice made Grace look at him. He met her gaze with a trembling smile as a tear rolled down his cheek.

"What a wonderful gift you've been given, Gracie. Thank you for sharing it with Lizzie. And with me." He made no effort to hide his emotion, just hugged his little girl close and pressed a kiss on her head.

"You're welcome." There was so much more Grace wanted to say, but her phone rang. "It's Jess. Excuse me. Hello," she said as she rose and walked down the steps and across the grass. She chose a lovely private spot under a huge cottonwood tree. "How are you, dear?"

"A little depressed," Jess responded, sounding sad. "Even though I've changed ships now, the camel-riding excursion is still full. I won't be able to participate."

"Oh, I'm so sorry, dear. I know how much you wanted to do that." Grace couldn't tear her gaze away from Jack and Lizzie on the deck. The two seemed to be having an in-depth discussion about something serious.

"It's okay. I'm making a mountain out of a molehill. I have no business complaining." Jess managed a laugh. "This trip is amazing enough even without that. What's up with you? How's the rodeo planning?"

"Everything is coming along well. Our ladies group has the food menu nailed down and I think Jack and Ben have most of the other items we discussed in order. The registrations are pouring in." She debated saying more, then decided to be honest. "Some of the various government agencies' requirements are costing more than we expected though. I've run the numbers and I doubt we'll be able to donate as much as we'd hoped."

"Oh, too bad." There was a pause before Jess asked, "How is Jack?"

"Um, okay. He's—different." Grace couldn't come up with a better descriptor.

"Different how? What do you mean?"

"I mean he's different. Not so brash and pushy, more thoughtful. He actually listens to me and sometimes even asks *me* to help *him*, instead of just telling me I'm going to." She smiled at the memories. "He's changed a lot since he first arrived, Jess," she admitted, thinking of the differences in him that she hadn't mentioned. Like his gentleness and his generosity of time.

"What happened?" Her friend wanted to know.

"I'm not certain, but I think it's tied up with his past. Remember the issues he had with his father when we were teens?"

"Yes, I do. He seemed so wounded back then." Her friend's voice was soft with reminiscence. "He tried hard to please, but his father was like a hunk of granite. Harsh."

"There was some enmity between them that I think Jack's carried for years. It's like he's now letting go of that." Grace didn't want to reveal any confidences so she added only, "He also had a terrible marriage."

"And yet he wants to marry you, to take the risk all over again?" Grace knew the question before Jess voiced it. "What have you decided about that?"

"I haven't decided." Grace sighed heavily. "I've prayed and prayed, but I feel no direction from God about my future."

"Well, what do you *feel* for Jack?"

"At first I disliked him a lot. Or at least the way he acted. He was arrogant and that annoyed me. But he's not the same anymore," she explained. "He was making excuses not to spend time with

Lizzie. Now it seems like he makes excuses to do things *with* her."

"Or maybe he wants to spend time with *you*," Jess suggested, her voice intimating romance. "Because he's realized what a spectacularly gorgeous, talented woman you are."

"Could be my new haircut." She laughed at Jess's groan. "Truthfully? Jack is quite attentive to me, too. With Lizzie now out of school, he insists on taking his turn caring for her. He claims I must have lots of time to do things on my own."

"What do you do on your own?"

"Not much but weed your garden." Grace laughed. "The three of us end up together most days. Lizzie always has a new list of stuff she wants to do. She's started riding again, did I tell you?"

"You're changing the subject but no, you didn't tell me that. When?"

"A few days ago. She just announced at breakfast that Jack and I needed to ask Mandy to let her ride a horse." Grace loved the memory of that day. "Apparently the Calhoun kids have been practicing for the rodeo and Lizzie felt left out."

"Whatever the reason, it's great."

"Yes, it is. I thought Jack would insist on hovering while she rode, but he didn't." Wonderment still filled Grace. "He lets Mandy do the teaching. Not that Lizzie needs much. She's a great little rider."

"Still, I'm guessing Jack kept watch, didn't he?"

"Yes, but from the log cabin deck," Grace agreed. "When I caught him, he told me he's a *recovering* controller. I was so proud of him for that."

"You've changed, too. I can hear it in your voice." Jess asked very quietly, "Are you in love with Jack, Grace?"

She'd asked herself that question a hundred times in the past month. She asked it every time his hand brushed hers or when he shared a murmured comment, or when he complimented her on something and her heart began to dance.

"Grace?"

"I don't know, Jess. I like him a lot, even more than I did when I was fifteen," she admitted.

"Wow! That is a lot," Jess teased. "So what's your issue?" She waited a moment then asked, "Are you afraid?"

"Of what?"

"Of letting go. Of not being the same old Grace Partridge that you've always been," she said, and then added, "Are you afraid of love?"

"Yes," she admitted honestly. "But why would I fear something I've been praying for my entire life?" Grace was desperate to understand herself.

"That's exactly why," Jess insisted. "Because it's new to you. Because love means letting go and you're afraid that if you do, Jack might not catch you?"

"Maybe I am," Grace admitted, to her friend and to herself.

"Then you need to remember a verse I read this morning. *There is no fear in love; but perfect love casteth out fear.*" The smile in her voice transmitted clearly, even from halfway across the world. "Love isn't for wimps, my friend. It takes courage and strength and perseverance. It's hard work, but it's so worth it. Give love a chance, Grace."

They talked a bit more before Jess had to end the call. Grace stayed where she was, thinking about her friend's comments and that she hadn't told Jess the whole truth.

Actually, she was head over heels in love with Jack Prinz.

But would he ever love her?

And was marriage to Jack part of God's plan for her?

Chapter Twelve

"Good night, Sweet Pea." Jack hugged Lizzie, delighting in the sweet scent of the freshly bathed little girl. "I love you," he whispered, thrilled to hear those words come from his own lips.

"I love you, too, Pops." Lizzie lay back to regard him with serious scrutiny. "You like your Father's Day gift, don't you?"

"I told you, darlin'. I love it." He preened for her in the red-and-black-checked shirt she'd given him. "How did you know red is my favorite color?"

"'Cause it was Daddy's favorite," she said with a big smile. Then her forehead creased. "Do you miss Daddy and Mommy, Pops?"

"Every single day, Sweet Pea." Jack brushed the dark hair away from her cheek and pressed a kiss there. "Are you still feeling scared I'll leave you?" he asked and then wondered if that was a good question to ask her.

He wished Grace had stayed nearby. She would have nudged him if he said the wrong thing and then comforted Lizzie. But she always left them for the last few minutes together, as if she knew he had years to make up for in this bedtime ritual. In Cade's younger years, Sheena had always made sure he was tucked in and asleep before Jack saw him. When he insisted, she'd angrily warn him not to wake the boy up or he'd pay. Maybe that's why Jack indulged himself with Lizzie. Cade had grown up so fast. So would she.

And then maybe it would be too late to tell Grace…

To every thing there is a season, Ecclesiastes says.

Pastor Ed's sermon from this morning echoed inside Jack's head.

Nobody knows how long or short a season we get, folks. That's why we need to enjoy everyone God gives us, to squeeze the most happiness we can from each moment. Nobody ever died from too much love, too much hand-holding or too much hugging. Go overboard with those you care about. Lavish them with kindness and generosity and love.

Isn't it better to be remembered for the time you spent sharing special moments in someone's life than to be remembered for money or things? Fill every season with joy.

"Pops, you're not listening." Lizzie's hand cupped his cheek and pressed so he would turn his head to her.

"Sorry, Sweet Pea." He refocused. "Tell me again, please."

"I said, sometimes I'm sad about Mommy and Daddy, and I think maybe you'll go away, too, but then I read the new book Miss P. made me 'bout sad and happy an' I feel better."

"A new book? How come I haven't seen it?" He wondered when Grace had time.

"You didn't ask," Lizzie said in gentle reproof. "Miss P. does lotsa stuff for us that you don't see, Pops."

"Yeah?" He thought he'd been very observant. "Like what?"

"She fixed my sweater that Mommy made me," Lizzie explained. "It was kinda wrecky and didn't fit so good, but Miss P. made it really nice an' now I c'n wear it lots, only not in summer time. But it's my favorite sweater," she said. "See it?" She pointed to the item folded on a chair. "It's got longer sleeves an' stuff."

He vaguely remembered once wanting to throw it out and Lizzie tearfully refusing because it reminded her of her mother. Now the precious article had been repaired and restored. By Grace.

"Miss P.'s makin' me another one for when I start first grade. She's really smart at makin' stuff."

"She sure is," he agreed.

"An' when she sings—oh, Pops, you should hear. She sings so nice. She thinks she isn't very good so she only sings if nobody's around, but it is so good." Lizzie yawned. "Tomorrow she's gonna teach me how to weed her friend's garden. I don't think I like weeding," she said, wrinkling her nose in distaste, "but Miss P. says you gotta take the good with the bad. Or somethin' like that."

"Miss P. is absolutely right, Sweet Pea. But I think you better stop talking about her now and go to sleep," Jack said softly. "Sweet dreams for a sweet pea."

"First I gotta say my prayers. Close your eyes, Pops." Lizzie yawned again, then began. "Dear God, thanks for a nice Father's Day and for getting Pops to like his shirt and for the yummy cookies. And thanks for getting Miss P. to help me get it even if it costs her lots of money. Maybe you could send her some more?"

Lots of money? Jack wanted to clap his hand to his head. He'd forgotten to set up some kind of account that Gracie could use to pay for Lizzie's expenses.

"Pops, you're s'posed to keep your eyes closed when we're prayin'," Lizzie scolded.

"Sorry. But you were looking, too," he teased. She glowered at him so he squeezed his eyes closed. "Go ahead, honey."

"God bless Pops an' Miss P. and all the Calhoun kids. I'm not sayin' all their names, God, 'cause there's lots an' I'm real tired." Lizzie opened one eye to check on him. Jack shut his eyes fast. "An' please take real good care of my mommy and daddy an' tell them I love them lots."

She stopped. Jack waited for her *amen* but it didn't come.

"Lizzie?" he whispered, wondering if she'd drifted off.

"Shh! There was something else I was gonna pray 'bout—oh, yeah. And please, God, help me think of a birthday present to get for Miss P. Amen." She pressed her head into the pillow with a dreamy smile and whispered, "Good night, Pops."

A second later, Lizzie's chest rose and fell in soft whiffling snores.

"Good night, my darling girl." Careful not to rouse her, Jack pressed one more kiss against her velvety cheek, then rose and left the room, quietly closing the door behind him while his brain stewed.

Grace's birthday? When was it? How could he find out, and what could he get for the amazing woman who'd rescued him and his granddaughter?

"Everything okay, Jack?" He found Grace sitting on the deck knitting.

"Yes. Why?" He sat down across from her.

"You're frowning." She looked at him, her face half-shadowed but accentuating her high cheekbones.

"I was thinking about your friend and how you said she can't seem to get on that camel ride she wants," he said, trying to come up with a way to ask about her birthday.

"It really is too bad. From the day we started planning this trip together, camel riding has been first on Jess's bucket list," Grace explained. "But when I realized I'd be going alone I canceled the reservation without even thinking about Jess. Camel riding is so *not* on *my* bucket list." She made a comical face at him.

"What is on your list?" Jack thought he'd never tire of looking at Grace Partridge. She personified her name—grace, elegance and poise, but with a dash of practicality that eliminated any possibility of her seeming aloof.

"Oh, it's under revision at the moment," she said airily.

"You look very beautiful sitting there in the gloaming, Gracie." He grinned when her head jerked upward and she stared at him in surprise.

"I'm not beautiful," she said with a frown.

"I think you're very beautiful," he insisted.

"Well, thank you, Jack. That's a very nice compliment."

"I don't know how you see to knit out here," he mused, surprised the yard light hadn't yet come on.

"No pattern in this. It's plain knitting, mostly by touch. Was Lizzie okay?" She flipped her needles and began working in the opposite direction.

"Tired, but happy. Thank you for helping her choose my shirt," he said. Tomorrow he'd talk to her about money, but not tonight. Money was too mundane a subject for a gorgeous evening like this. "She said you made her another book. May I see it?"

"If you like. It's in there." She pointed to Lizzie's special box nestled on a shelf against the wall. "I was hoping to help her see that the special things her parents taught her are lessons she can use with others." She made a face. "Also, I wanted to polish the last book but she wouldn't let me change anything, so I needed a new project."

Jack paged through her work, once more impressed by the way she had blended Lizzie's grief and loss with memories of tenderness and love and joy.

"These are fantastic watercolors, Gracie," he said, awed by her ability to answer Lizzie's questions and soothe her sorrow by combining God's love with gentle words. "There's such—" He struggled to find the appropriate word. "Charm and beauty in the way you've put this together. Any child would love a book like this. Are you now pursuing publication?"

"No." She tilted her head to one side and shrugged. Her lips curved in a self-deprecating smile. "I'm too busy. I was more regimented about writing every day when I was at the library."

"You shouldn't give it up," Jack said and meant it as he closed the little book and returned it to Lizzie's box. "I'm sure there are a lot of children who would be deeply moved by work like this."

"It's nice of you to say, Jack, but—"

"I mean it," he insisted. "I've seen Lizzie having a sad day and then she remembers your first book. She reads the words, touches the pictures and it gives her great peace. It's incredibly moving to see the impact of your work."

"Thank you." She stopped then and returned her knitting to the bag she carried it in.

"Don't let me interrupt you," he said.

"You're not. I want to watch the sky." She exhaled and stretched her arms upward. "This ranch is glorious, isn't it? I'm so glad I get to spend part of the summer here. Just smell that freshly mown hay, Jack. And listen to the birds."

"Does this mean you're glad Lizzie and I came?" he asked, half joking but intensely curious about her answer.

"I am," she said, surprising him. "Lizzie is a darling. I would have missed a lot not knowing her."

"And me?" Jack felt like a stupid kid as he waited on tenterhooks for her response. "Are you glad we met again?"

"I am. Very." Grace's serious expression told him it was true. "I wondered about you for years, how you were doing, *what* you were doing. It's been good to reconnect."

"Sounds like a farewell speech." And he didn't like it. "Are you trying to say *here's your hat, what's your hurry*?"

"Of course not! I would never—"

"Relax, Grace. I was teasing. You have too much tact to even hint at something so crass."

But sooner or later we will have to leave. Why did he find that so distasteful? Because he would miss this woman and the fun they had together. And yet, he could hardly stay if there would be no more intimate relationship between them. That would be too hard.

"Aren't you going to tell me again that I need to marry you?" She sounded—what? Like she wanted to accept? *Don't delude yourself, Jack.*

"No, I'm not telling you that again," he decided on the spot. If he told her he had feelings for her and she rejected him... "I'm not telling you that ever again."

"Oh." Funny how that sounded like disappointment?

Jack shook his head to clear it.

"May I ask you why not?" Grace sat perfectly still with her chin tilted down so he couldn't read her eyes. As if she was afraid to hear what he said?

"I've already asked you to marry me. Many times," he reminded her. "Ed's sermon on that verse in Ecclesiastes, the one about seasons, has really made me think about timing. Maybe the timing isn't right for you, for us."

"I see." The whispered response didn't give him any clue about her reactions.

The next part was hard to say because Jack was used to *doing* things, not waiting for someone else to make decisions. But the deeper his Bible study with Ben went, the more he realized that some things just couldn't be forced. Especially marriage. He was pretty sure that was a lesson he should have learned a long time ago.

"The thing is, Gracie, you already know all my reasons for wanting to marry you. Nothing's changed about that. *I* haven't changed."

Liar! The voice in his head screamed so loudly, he checked to see if she'd heard it. *Everything's changed. Except that you still don't know how to deal with what you're feeling about Gracie Partridge. Because you're still afraid to risk being vulnerable.*

Yes, he was! Because vulnerable people got hurt!

You don't trust.

"You and Lizzie are leaving then?" Would she be sad if he did?

"I told you I'd stay until the rodeo's over and then leave, unless you decided to marry me. I keep my promises." He rose, captured her hands in his and drew her upward to stand in front of him. He met her purple gaze and smiled, unable to help himself from touching her cheek, smoothing a wayward curl against her brow. "I haven't changed my mind about marrying you, Gracie. I still want that, more than ever. But I'm not going to pressure you. It's your decision."

She stood in the moonlight, looking elegantly polished in her white jeans and dark indigo shirt.

Her smile was tremulous, as if she was trying to control her emotions. Jack didn't like that. He loved her unfettered joy and exuberance in life, loved seeing her beautiful eyes light up and watching her mobile lips break into an uncontainable smile.

"My future is up to you, Gracie." Jack bent his head and touched his lips to hers. "Good night."

He'd intended only the lightest of kisses. But then his arm found its way around her waist and her hand brushed against his chest before sliding around his neck to draw him closer as her lips returned his kiss, and asked for more. Suddenly a simple good-night kiss turned into the kind of tender embrace he'd only ever dreamed about when he dreamed of her.

Gracie was so special, so—*dear*. He desperately wanted for her to believe that to him she was the most beautiful, amazing woman who had so much to give. He deepened their kiss, drawing her yet closer as he poured the words he couldn't say into actions.

He was lost in a world totally focused on Gracie—until she gently eased away from him.

"Good night, Jack. Have a good rest," she whispered as her lips brushed his ear. Then she went inside the little log house he now thought of as her home.

Jack made his way down the stairs carefully, but he didn't go to the main house. Instead, he sat at *their* picnic table and watched the sky unfold its starry spread while he faced the realization that he now wanted to marry Gracie more than he ever had.

Because he loved her?

Of course you love her. Who wouldn't? The entire town of Sunshine adores her.

But was it really love that he felt? What was he supposed to do if she did agree to marry him? Risk it? Protect himself? Turn her down?

You're an idiot, Jack Prinz. The real question is, what if she won't marry you? What if you lose Grace from your life? What then?

Irritated by the rush of dismay that filled him at that thought, Jack forgot about the stars and walked toward the main house. Despite the inner taunting, he wasn't totally confident he *did* love Gracie. Maybe he was trying to recapture the past. Maybe he only thought she was special because of all the things she'd done for Lizzie and him.

Maybe he was just starved for affection.

Whatever Jack called it, love or a very good friendship, the bottom line was, he couldn't stomach the thought of Grace rejecting him. Not now. Not after all they'd gone through, all he'd come to know about her, to trust her, to enjoy spending time with her.

It was time to do something loving for Gracie that would show he cared about her, like Pastor Ed had said. Maybe then she would love him.

The little books she'd made were amazing, like nothing he'd even seen when he'd been searching for a way to talk to Lizzie about her parents' deaths. Was there some way Jack could organize a birthday gift Gracie would never forget?

A gift big enough to make her love him?

"This rodeo is really something, isn't it, Gracie?" Jack said, eyes sparkling and that unforgettable smile dazzling her.

"It really is," she agreed as she handed over yet another glass of lemonade. "The weather is perfect and Bonnie and Ben have made everyone so welcome on the Double H. Even Pastor Ed managed to get his coffee booth set up."

"He's doing pretty well, too." He glanced around, seemed to notice the food booth wasn't particularly busy. "Can you take a break? Sweet Pea is supposed to ride in a few minutes," he said, hearing his own anxiety. "I thought we could watch her together."

"I've been waiting for that." Grace excused herself to the other ladies in their temporary booth and stepped from behind the counter, patting her hair while thoughts of his kisses filled her head.

"You look amazing, as usual." Jack was always complimenting her. Many others had said she was glowing. Because of Jack.

"Hey, slow down a bit, cowboy." She slid her hand into his so he couldn't get too far ahead of her.

She'd grown comfortable with his touch, mostly because he'd taken to kissing her goodnight, and good morning come to think of it, and would not be denied, even if Lizzie was watching.

"My legs are shorter than yours," she reminded him.

"Mmm-hmm." He gave her jeans-clad legs an appreciative glance and then winked at her. "I like them that way." She blushed but doubted he noticed since his attention quickly swerved back to the riding ring.

"Why aren't you with Lizzie?" She shook her head at him. "You know you want to be."

"More than just about anything," Jack agreed, drawing her onto a riser so they could see the participants. "But Mandy's her teacher, not me. And Lizzie wants us to watch from here."

She felt sorry for him, knowing how much he wanted to hover and protect his granddaughter. But he also wanted Lizzie to recapture the joy she'd once found in riding with her parents and this was a good way to start.

The benches were crowded. Jack edged right up beside her, his arm across her back for support. Grace pretended not to notice how close they were, but in her heart, she was truly enjoying these moments together.

"We should have brought a drink—Jack?" Grace frowned. His eyes were closed but they opened just enough to look at her. "Are you all right?"

"Fine. Just saying a word for Sweet Pea." He took the white Stetson she was holding and set it on her head. "The sun's hot. We don't want to burn that gorgeous skin." Then he ducked his head under the brim and kissed her.

"Jack!" Grace had to restrain herself from responding. "Everyone will see."

"And not one single man here will question my kissing such a beautiful woman," he said and grinned at her blush.

"Is that her? Where did she get that red-checkered shirt from?" Grace asked to distract him.

"Me. It goes with her red boots, don't you think?" Jack frowned. "Oh no. Her group is first in barrel racing. She likes jumping better."

"But she didn't enter in that. She'll do fine, Jack," Grace leaned closer to whisper.

"I know. But…" He looked at her with such pathos that she slid her hand in his and wove their fingers together. "I'm being stupid, aren't I?"

"You're being her pops," Grace said gently. "Nothing wrong with that." She so wanted to support him in his new attitude. "Can you tell me about barrel racing? I've seen it done, of course, but I've never paid much attention to what the rules are."

"It's simple. The horse and rider attempt to run a cloverleaf pattern around those barrels in the fastest possible time, without going out of their lanes or knocking over a barrel," he explained. "There are penalties for doing each."

"Okay." She studied each of the horses lined up in the back field. They looked so large compared to the children riding them. "What is it supposed to demonstrate?"

"The horse's athletic ability and the horseman-ship skills of the rider," Jack said. He smiled and Grace's heart started that staccato beat again.

"Thanks," she murmured.

"Anytime, Gracie." His fingers tightened around hers before he released them. "There she goes. Mandy chose a good mount. Lizzie sits that pinto really well. Okay, first barrel. Atta girl, Sweet Pea!"

Grace echoed Jack's words in her head, but she couldn't say anything. She was too focused on the way Lizzie guided her mount around the second barrel and then raced for home.

"Oh, well done," she cheered.

"Her time will be a bit slow," Jack murmured, studying the shot he'd just taken on his camera.

"Who cares?" Grace demanded with a glare. "She did it."

"I know, sweetheart." He pretend-bumped her shoulder with his. "I'm just sayin' she needs to speed up on the second try."

Shocked by the *sweetheart*, Grace managed to ask, "Why?"

"To win!"

"Jack!" she scolded. "It's not about Lizzie winning or losing. It's about—"

"I know," he interrupted softly, his voice tinged with sadness. "But she's lost so much lately. I just want her to have a win in something."

"We'll celebrate no matter what," Grace promised, deeply moved by his compassion for his granddaughter. "Who's next?"

"Two of the Calhoun kids are racing now. See how Mandy's watching Ella. Hard not to cheer for your own kid."

Grace sat beside him and thought how wonderful it was to share this with him. Such simple moments, and yet, she would remember them for the rest of her life, long after Jack was gone.

Because she couldn't marry him. She knew that now. Since Jack had arrived, God had been trying to show her that too much time had passed, too many things had changed, especially Jack. She wanted too much from him. She wanted to be his true sweetheart, wanted to have first place in his heart and wanted to hear him say he loved her. But he didn't. Or couldn't. And she'd refused to accept that, kept hoping, praying, repeatedly asking God when she knew He was saying no.

Okay then, Grace vowed as she stared clear-eyed at the track. She wouldn't have a future with a man who did not love her. But she had today, and maybe tomorrow with Jack. She would make the best of whatever days were left. She'd savor every moment, squeeze out every ounce of joy, and most of all, she'd have no regrets.

"Here comes our girl."

Oh, Jack, how I wish she truly was ours. How I wish we could share all of her special moments, that I'd be there to see when she graduates, when you walk her down the aisle, when we laugh and joke together and pat ourselves on the back for being such good grandparents.

"Gracie?" Jack touched her chin, pressing up so she would look at him. "Are you sick?"

"No," she told him with a smile. "Just daydreaming."

"Lizzie's ready to go again." He stood as the whistle sounded and began taking pictures. "Go, girl," he mumbled with admirable restraint.

Grace kept her eyes on Lizzie, who was bent low in the saddle as the horse galloped up to the barrel. She leaned in, anticipating his turn, but he skidded in the sand. Everyone gasped as the little girl tipped far to one side, her leg almost grazing the ground.

"Hang on, Lizzie," Grace whispered. "No matter what, hang on." She grabbed Jack's hand and felt the reassuring pressure of his fingers against hers.

"She can do it," he said, but his voice quavered.

A second later, the horse had regained his footing. He sped around the barrel and raced for the finish line with Lizzie slapping the reins against his neck and yelling encouragement. A great roar went out from the crowd as the little girl crossed the chalk line first.

"Oh, my." Grace fanned her face as she tried to catch her breath.

"No kidding." Jack sat down beside her but didn't release her hand. "What's her time?"

Grace was hardly able to breathe until at last the announcer gave the times.

"She's won her heat. But did she win the race?" Jack let go of her fingers to rise again, as if he could see what was happening. It seemed as if they waited a year for the final results.

"Winner of the six-and-under barrel racing is Keena Thompkins. Second goes to Lizzie Prinz. Third to Amanda Bell."

"Lizzie won second, Jack. She won second!" Delighted, Grace threw her arms around him and hugged for all she was worth. She felt Jack's arms slide around her waist and didn't care one whit that everyone could see, or that by tomorrow the whole of Sunshine would be gossiping about them. Again.

"Yes, she did," he said. His grin was huge. "Not bad for her first time out."

"Let's go congratulate her."

"Okay." He held her hand as they navigated their way out of the stands.

Jack accepted folks' congratulations with a grin and a wave but Grace kept her focus on where she was going. Hugging Jack was one thing. Doing a face-plant in front of everyone—that was something else entirely.

They were out of the stands when Jack's phone rang. He listened and then promised to come immediately.

"Sorry, darlin', but there's an issue with the bouncy house in the meadow," he apologized with an eye roll. "Kids are bawling. Parents are frustrated. I gotta go fix it." He bent down and brushed his lips against hers. "I'll find you later."

"Jack, you can't keep kissing—" Oh, what was the point when she liked him kissing her? "Later," she agreed and watched him hurry away, dodging in and out of groups as well as he could with his booted foot.

She made it to Lizzie in time to see her awarded her ribbon.

"You were amazing, dear. Just amazing."

"Thanks. Where's Pops? Did he see me?" The little girl glanced around, though she didn't seem overly worried by Jack's absence.

"Did he see you? He nearly burst his buttons watching you. We are so proud of you." Grace hugged her tightly. "I know you have to go curry your horse now and give him some oats. And you have that parade event. Do you want me to come with you until it's time?"

"Nah. Drew said he'll take me to the food

booth where you're working when I'm finished. I didn't even ask him to do it."

Drew, who stood behind her, nodded. "No worries, Miss P."

"The rodeo's a success, isn't it?" she asked him sotto voce.

"A huge one." His grin sparkled in the sun. "We even got a giant donation. We're going to make a big dent in redoing that camp pool as well as complete our other items. God has really blessed this event." He waggled his hand at her, then left with Lizzie.

"You gave that donation, Jack," she murmured to herself as she found her apron and stored her Stetson. "You and your big soft heart. So why can't you love me?"

And then she remembered. Now that the rodeo was over, Jack and Lizzie would leave.

Chapter Thirteen

Jack avoided the *thank-you* part of the rodeo's closing ceremonies. He didn't need or want anyone's thanks because he'd been blessed beyond measure by both the rodeo and his time on this ranch. He'd received much more than he'd given.

It was late by the time the guests were gone, things were taken down, removed or replaced, and the ranch was back to normal. He was weary, but he had to stop by to kiss Lizzie good-night. And to see Grace.

Today had been a day he'd only ever dreamed of, full of happiness and joy. Because Grace was with him. They'd laughed so much, especially as they shared the very last piece of lemon pie when she'd mocked him for getting meringue all over his face. Jack didn't care about that. He just wanted to be with her, to hear her sweet laughter bubble out, to share each precious moment.

As he climbed the stairs, the anticipation of seeing Grace again took his breath away. He tapped very softly on the log house door. It opened a moment later.

"Hi. Come to see Lizzie?" Grace motioned him

inside. "I think she's drifted off already, but go ahead in."

"You look—stunning," was the only descriptive he could think of. She was covered from head to toe in a shimmery silver dress, no, caftan, he thought it was called. "You look like a princess," he said, unable to tear his gaze away.

"Thank you. Jess sent it. After I opened it, I couldn't resist trying it on." She nudged him farther inside and closed the screen door. "My dear friend is flying pretty high at the moment. They organized a second excursion to the camels and she was able to go." She tilted her head to the side, her gaze coolly assessing. "I think you made that possible, didn't you, Jack?"

"Me?" He pretended surprise. "How would I know how to arrange that or even what ship she's on?"

"I haven't yet figured out how you did it, and maybe that doesn't really matter." Grace's voice wasn't soft and intimate, as it had been earlier today. More businesslike? But perhaps that was because she was as tired as he was. "Just know that we both appreciate it very much. Jess is never going to forget that ride."

"I doubt she'll forget any of her wonderful trip," he said, wondering why it felt like a barrier had somehow come between them since they'd shared that pie. "When does she return?"

"In a week, the day after my birthday. I can

hardly wait to see her." Grace fell silent, as if she couldn't think of anything else to say to him.

"I'm sure you've missed her."

"Yes." The easy banter of this afternoon was completely gone.

Something had changed with Gracie.

"Well, I'll just poke my head in to see Lizzie, if that's okay?"

"Of course." She picked up her knitting bag and went to sit on the deck.

Jack hesitated, wondering if he should ask what was wrong. But he had a hunch that whatever was bothering Grace was private. With a resigned sigh, he went to see Lizzie. He smiled at how she lay sprawled across the bed, her winning ribbon pinned to the teddy bear she adored and now clutched in one hand.

Jack brushed his hand over the glossy black curls, soaking in the feel of her tender skin, watching her chest rise and fall in soft whiffling breaths, his heart welling with love like he'd never known he could feel.

"Oh, Sweet Pea, I love you so much," he whispered, content to gaze at her while his heart overflowed.

And then, in the silence of those precious moments, the sound of someone quietly weeping intruded. Jack frowned. It couldn't be Grace because she was on the deck at the front of the log house. Lizzie's bedroom was at the side. Then the gauzy window curtains billowed and sagged and he realized the window must be open, allowing sounds from the deck just around the corner to be heard.

Jack ached to rush out, take Grace in his arms and demand to know how he could make her world better. What could he do to stop those heart-rending, half-muffled sobs?

But he didn't move a muscle. Because Grace was a very proud and private woman. If she wanted his help, she'd ask. And she hadn't asked. Butting in would only embarrass her.

"Please, Lord, heal my heart. Take away the sadness." Her poignant whispered words faded as the prayer continued on too quietly for him to understand the rest.

Jack waited a long time, until fatigue and an aching foot demanded he find his own rest. At last he bent, kissed Lizzie's cheek and then walked out of the room. Aside from a small lamp burning on an end table, all the interior lights were off. So were those on the deck. He didn't turn them on. It was obvious Gracie wanted privacy. She said nothing from her darkened solitude as he exited the house.

"It was an amazing rodeo, Grace. Thank you so much for all your hard work and for sharing it with me." Jack struggled to say more. He didn't want to leave her like this; he ached to tell her how much he appreciated her help, how much he appreciated her.

"Don't thank me. You did most of the work, Jack." Her voice sounded scratchy, as if her throat was sore. "I think everyone had a good time and the children at camp will really appreciate the changes that money will allow to be made. Especially with the bonus donation you added."

He ignored that. What was money? Nothing compared to people.

"It was my pleasure to work with you," he murmured. "I'm sure you're as tired as I am, so I'll be going now. Good night. And I can't say it often enough, but thank you again for caring for Lizzie. That's a debt we'll never be able to repay."

"I don't want to be paid—" She stopped. It was a moment before she spoke again, this time in a ragged whisper. "Good night, Jack."

He wanted to say something, anything that would ease the pain she was going through. If he could just hold her—but he knew that would lead to an embrace and that would be unfair because he would not, could not tell her that he cared for her. Because he desperately feared that if he dared tell her what his heart felt, she would reject him.

"Please go, Jack," she begged.

"Good night." He left the little log cabin, alone and totally aware that it was his own fault that she'd grown cold toward him. After all, he'd let fear master him.

He'd stay a little longer, until the doctor gave his okay. But the day after Gracie's birthday, when her friend returned, it would be time to leave this place.

* * *

Over the next week, Grace kept as busy as possible. She spent hours perfecting the display in Jess's house and gardens, including manicuring the lawns better than any gardener could have. She tended to odd jobs in her own yard, too, to her renter's surprise. She took Lizzie with her on visits to the seniors' home and taught her how to cork knit. She took her charge to Peace Meadow often, knowing that it would be more difficult for Lizzie's grandfather to follow them there.

Anything to avoid the man who held her heart.

Grace could hardly bear to look at Jack now, to see that charming smile of his flash when he teased Lizzie, to watch him laugh with Ben as they studied their Bibles or to follow his limping gait as he checked out the ranch animals.

She so desperately wanted to escape, to have hours and days alone so she could search for a way to end the pain of knowing her dream was finally dead. To finally accept that there would be no happily-ever-after for Grace Partridge with Jack Prinz.

Mostly she was lonely. So lonely. There were always people around. But it was the yearning to be loved as she loved, to share the mundane with one who cared, to know that when she returned home, tired and careworn, her very special love would be waiting to comfort, to support and to pray with.

Not going to happen, Grace.

"I know now that marriage is not Your will for me," she prayed. "Please help me to accept it. Please give me a new task, a new interest, something to focus on so I can forget him."

As if!

Jack was unforgettable.

"Where are you going?" Lizzie demanded a week later when Grace picked up her bag and headed for the door.

"I'm going to run some errands," Grace explained. "Don't worry, your pops can make your toast-and-peanut-butter breakfast."

"Uh-uh." Lizzie shook her head firmly in a negative manner, lifted the handbag out of her hands and led her to the big easy chair in front of the window. "You hafta sit here."

Jack saw a frown wrinkle Grace's forehead and hurriedly intervened.

"Lizzie and I want to wish you a very happy birthday, Grace." He'd pretty much dropped her nickname this last week. It suited the distance he felt had come between them. This remote woman seemed less like Gracie, more like Grace as each interaction between them grew stiffer, more formal, less comfortable.

"Pops an' me got your whole birthday planned, Miss P.," Lizzie announced sternly. "That means you can't go do some dumb old errands. Not on your birthday."

"But I—"

"Stay there," Lizzie ordered. She scooted out the door and returned carrying a vase full to the brim with dandelions. "You said you liked these, 'member?"

"I love them." Grace's smile was almost back to the one Jack loved. "Thank you, dear." But when she glanced at him her smile faded. "I'm not really sure—"

"Me an' Pops are sure, aren't we, Pops?" How would he tell her they were leaving tomorrow? Where would they go?

"Listen, Sweet Pea," he said gently. "If Grace has things she'd rather do on her birthday, we need to respect that. You and I can do the things on our list, together."

"But that won't be as much fun!"

The child was right. Jack shrugged helplessly at Grace.

"What are these 'things' you have planned?" she asked in a resigned tone.

"First we're goin' to have a lumberjack birthday breakfast at, uh, someplace," Lizzie spread her hands, palms up. "I dunno what a lumberjack is or what they eat, but I guess if we don't like it, we c'n always have toast." She grinned cheerfully. "Come on, Miss. P.! I'm hungry. An' we're goin' in Pops's car 'cause he got his boot off yesterday."

Jack saw Grace glance at his foot in wide-eyed surprise. It pained him that she hadn't noticed earlier. Because she didn't care? Her gaze lit on his face before it darted away again, as if he was a stranger who held no importance in her life. In fact, during this entire past week, while tiptoeing around her, he'd felt like an outsider. Which he hated. In Jack's entire life, all he'd ever wanted was to belong somewhere. To someone. He thought he'd found that place here, where Grace was.

Okay, so maybe he didn't actually belong on this ranch. Maybe he *was* the outsider from Texas. But Lizzie did belong with Grace. They were two kindred souls.

Jack had prayed longer and harder this week than ever before in his life and he'd almost garnered enough courage to tell Grace he loved her. Almost. But in the wee hours, doubt and fear in the form of Sheena's voice kept filling his head, mocking him, reminding him of his failures as a husband, a father, and of the times he'd messed up with Lizzie. Telling him over and over that nobody would love him. Then his father's voice chimed in, calling him unlovable.

Jack kept reminding himself that it was a lie, that God loved him. That he was free of the past. But he wasn't totally convinced.

His marriage had been a complete disaster. Maybe it could be different with Grace. But maybe it wouldn't. Marrying Grace would be for life. There would be no divorce, because she didn't believe in it. It wasn't that he planned to be a failure again, but that voice reminding him that he was unlovable just wouldn't be silenced. It said Grace would never be able to love him. That possibility was daunting.

He'd almost convinced himself he could live without her love because he loved her enough for both of them. But would that love survive if she laughed at him or rejected him? Fear held his tongue silent. Telling Grace he loved her was a risk and Jack didn't do risk. Even though he prayed for help, even though he'd almost silenced the reminders of his father's denigrating comments, he just couldn't summon enough faith in God's love to take the leap.

"Hey, Jack. Wake up." The birthday girl had risen, picked up her handbag and was staring at him, as was Lizzie. "You're driving. Right?"

Maybe he couldn't tell her, but he could give Gracie the best birthday ever.

"Sorry, daydreaming." He held the door for his ladies and followed them outside where his new car waited. It *was* a fine car, but it paled in importance beside the very fine lady who was getting into the front seat. "Fasten your seat belts, girls. It's going to be a glorious day."

"Uh-huh." Grace rolled her eyes. He closed

her door, refusing to hear any more negatives. *For Lizzie's sake*, he told himself.

The drive into Sunshine was filled with his granddaughter's happy chatter. That was okay with Jack. He couldn't have said anything anyway. Grace's cool silence was more effective than a gag at their lumberjack breakfast, making it a mediocre success at best. Maybe he'd strike out with the planned outdoor museum visit, too.

"Can you walk in those shoes?" He frowned as she swung her elegant sandals out of his car.

"It has long been a practice of mine to only buy shoes in which I can walk, Jack," she shot back in a sassy tone. A tiny smile had begun to play with her lips.

They wandered around the grounds for several hours, learning some local history, indulging in a game of old-fashioned croquet and sipping freshly-squeezed lemonade on the beautiful grounds. An historic white-steepled church boasted a vintage spinet piano which Grace was persuaded to play. After some very off-key notes and many squeaks, she produced a semimusical version of "Happy Birthday" to accompany Jack's and Lizzie's singing.

"Time for lunch," Jack announced, directing them back to his vehicle.

"Not a lumberjack lunch, is it?" Gracie murmured with an uplifted brow and a quizzical expression when he drove downtown.

"No. Wait here. I'll just be a minute," Jack said as he parked the car.

"What is the man doing?" he heard her ask Lizzie.

"Wait and see, Miss Partridge," he muttered to himself as he ducked inside Joy Calhoun's bakery. "You just wait and see what I have planned."

They left the bakery and drove for quite a while.

"Are you sure you want to keep driving your brand-new car on this horribly rutted, gravel road?" Grace finally asked rather peevishly.

"I'm sure." It *was* taking forever to get there. Jack had just begun to question whether he'd taken the wrong road when the waterfall appeared.

"Oh, my." Grace's jaw dropped. "I've lived here all my life. How is it I've never seen this place?"

"This is a private estate, the work of one Herman Schneider, a bachelor engineer, who, being lonely for his countrymen, and women," he added quickly, "has decided to move back to his native Germany as soon as he sells this place." Jack parked and shut off the engine. "Can your very attractive shoes handle this grass?"

Grace shot him a droll look and stepped out of the car.

He picked up the bakery package and grabbed an old blanket he'd brought along, before leading them to an idyllic grassy spot shaded by three gorgeous aspen trees and bordered by flowers. He spread the blanket and then invited them to sit down.

"Your birthday feast, madame," Jack announced.

"This is— It's amazing! What a setting." Grace craned her neck to investigate her surroundings. "That house looks like a castle," she mused looking awestruck.

"It *is* a castle, as designed by Herman. We can tour it later if you like," Jack offered. "He gave me the key so I could water his plants while he's away on business."

"I would really enjoy seeing inside," she murmured. "Thank you."

Jack thought perhaps her icy facade was beginning to thaw.

"Look at our party plates and glasses," Lizzie begged, not to be outdone. "Me an' Pops picked them out specially for your birthday."

"They're so pretty." Grace smoothed Lizzie's dark pigtails and straightened the bows on them. "Thank you for thinking of me, dear."

"Welcome." Lizzie stood by Jack, accepting each thing he handed her as she announced the contents. "We got—what do you call them, Pops?"

"Croissants," he said.

"Yeah, them. An' some kinda meat." She looked at it and shrugged. "I dunno what it is."

"Black Forest ham." Jack gave Grace an eye roll.

"My favorites!" Grace accepted each package

as if it was the best gift she could have been given. "How did you know I love dill pickles?"

"Uh oh. This cheese has holes in it," Lizzie announced with a frown.

"It's Swiss cheese, dear, and it is delish with ham and croissants." Grace's purple eyes darkened as they rested on Jack. "You've gone overboard for me. Thank you."

"My pleasure. After our riparian buffet," he said in a television presenter's voice, then leaned in and added, "I heard it called that on television." Then he continued the showmanship spiel. "After our riparian buffet, we shall dabble our feet in the cool water and study Mr. Schneider's amazing waterfall."

They lunched in the sunshine and laughed at Lizzie's goofy jokes. And slowly Grace began to thaw just a little. She smiled and her joyous laughter echoed across the estate. She insisted on dipping her feet in the stream, grinning when Lizzie squealed at the coldness of it. Later, when they'd returned to their sunspot under the trees to dry off, Jack fetched a birthday cake he'd stowed in a carrier in the trunk.

He and Lizzie sang "Happy Birthday" as loudly as they could, striving to outdo each other in volume if not quite in harmony.

"Quite a rousing rendition," Grace commended. She giggled at the corkscrew candles he set on the cake and then fell silent when he lit them.

"Isn't it pretty, Miss P.?"

"It really is, Lizzie. And I can't tell you how delighted I am that your grandfather didn't get one candle for every year."

"Oh, dear, no," Jack said with a grin when she'd blown them out. "That would be going overboard."

"And you never do that, right?" She wagged her finger back and forth.

"Never." He pretended to look around. "Where's that ice-cream truck and the clowns I ordered? Never mind. Let's go look through the engineer's house. You can help me water the plants."

He loved her laughter. He loved this fun, this warm sharing with Grace. He loved Grace.

Why couldn't he trust God enough to believe she could love him?

If only he dared to risk it…

Chapter Fourteen

"I don't believe I've ever had such a wonderful, amazing, fantastic birthday." Grace sank into the chair on the deck and watched the sun sink under the horizon. "Thank you so much, Jack."

"It was my very great pleasure," he said in the quietest, most solemn voice she'd ever heard from him. "But it's not quite over." He exhaled. "I have something for you, Grace. I only hope you won't be angry at me for taking liberties."

"What liberties?" She frowned and straightened up in her chair. "We should have kept Lizzie up so she could watch."

"You can tell her tomorrow."

When he remained standing there, she finally cleared her throat, her uncertainty obvious in her softly spoken, "Jack?"

"I need to say something first, Grace. I'm trying to get it said right."

"Take your time." The solemnity of his voice worried her, but she held her tongue fearing he was going to say goodbye.

"Those books you wrote and illustrated for Lizzie." He lifted his head and stared into her eyes. "They're the most beautiful watercolor pictures combined with precious thoughtful words that I've ever seen. They are the reason why Lizzie is beginning to accept her parents' deaths, to be less clingy and to learn more about God. You have made a tremendous difference in her life, Grace."

"Thank you." Was that it? He wanted to thank her for the books before they left? That was her birthday gift?

"Because I was so impressed with your work and so proud of how much it helped Lizzie, I borrowed the second book you wrote."

"Borrowed it?" She frowned. "Why?"

"I sent it to someone." He gulped and avoided her surprised stare as he continued. "A friend of Milt's."

"Oh." Grace couldn't think of anything else to say, so she sat there, waiting.

"And this friend has written a letter saying he would like to publish your work."

The bald statement took her by surprise. At first she couldn't make sense of it. Then—

"Publish?" she whispered in disbelief. "Milt's friend is a publisher?"

"Heart Publishing. He owns it." Jack fumbled as he drew a letter from his pocket. "His name is Grant Archer. He was a street kid, like me, that Milt took in. Grant never forgot that, or Milt. He used to visit Milt's ranch several times a year."

"I see." She swallowed, trying to soothe her dry throat. "That's interesting."

"The thing is, Gracie, he wants to buy your book." When she simply stared at him, Jack added, "To publish it. But there's a caveat."

Grace couldn't make it sink in.

"Grant wants more than two books from you," Jack explained. "He wants you to create a whole series of books that will help children understand the painful and confusing times in their lives with a godly perspective. He wants them to be as helpful as the two you wrote for Lizzie."

Stunned, afraid to believe what she'd heard, Grace rose and paced across the deck, trying to make sense of it. Only it didn't make sense.

"Heart Publishing is the *premiere* children's publisher in this country, Jack," she enunciated clearly. "They don't just go around offering multibook deals to new writers."

"I know, Grace. But that is what Grant's offering you." Jack held her stare, a faint smile curving the corners of his mouth. "I just got caught in the middle."

"You must have misunderstood," she said shaking her head.

"I don't think so." He held out the letter. "Happy birthday, Grace."

She opened the envelope and lifted out the sheet. It took seconds to read the words, but minutes for reality to penetrate. Her, a published author? But that's what it said.

Joy burst inside Grace. Here at last was God's answer to her prayer, part of it anyway, to be used in His service. At least she could live one dream she'd given up on. That Jack had done this for her—she was overwhelmed by his generosity.

Without thought she flew across the deck, flung her arms around him and pressed her lips to his in a kiss that he took forever to respond to. But all too soon he was pulling away.

"Gracie, I—"

"I love you, Jack Prinz." She kissed him again, unable to keep silent any longer.

"Wh-what did you say?" He stared at her dumbfounded.

"I said I love you," she repeated joyfully. "I have since I was fifteen, but a lot more now. I love you with every fiber of my being and if—"

"Wait!" Jack cupped her face in his hands and studied her for several long moments. Then he closed his eyes and whispered, "Okay, I'm trusting You."

Confused, she could only stare at him. Her mouth fell open when, holding both her hands, he knelt before her.

"Jack, what are—"

"Grace Partridge, I love you for a thousand different reasons which I'll happily go into later. For now, know that I'm ashamed to say I didn't trust God enough to tell you that earlier and let Him work out the rest. I thought it was too risky, that you might reject me and, well, as you know, I've had a bellyful of rejection."

"You mean you wimped out." Grace's dark gaze dared him to deny it.

"Well, I wouldn't put it that way." One look at her face and he nodded. "Yes, okay. I wimped out, with you and with God. But that's not ever happening again. I love you. I want to marry you. I want you by my side for the rest of my life. And I'm not going anywhere until you say you'll be there."

"Well, I'm not getting on my knees to tell you so get up, Jack!" She tugged on his arm until he was standing and then she drew him closer. "Naturally I'm going to marry you," she assured him with a cheeky grin. "Haven't you paid any attention to the gossip about me? I'm a very practical woman, and turning you down would certainly not be practical when I love you so much."

"Uh, Gracie?"

"Yes?"

"No offense, but be quiet now and kiss me."

"Yes, dear."

When they'd finally reassured each other that their love was mutual, they sat together on the porch swing, holding hands and sorting through all the unasked questions each had for the other.

"I've known Grant Archer for years, but when

he called me yesterday, I wasn't expecting his questions." Jack fiddled with her empty ring finger.

"What did he want to know?"

"He asked me if Grace Partridge was the kind of woman who lived the faith she presented in her books." Jack brushed a kiss against her chin.

"What did you say?"

"I told him I'd seen firsthand how fully you live out your faith. I said you were my inspiration for renewing my own faith journey, even though I'm nowhere near where I should be." He shook his head at her. "But at least I'm not where I was. I've made so many mistakes, Gracie. Most of them because I believed a lie and wouldn't take a risk on the truth. I wouldn't trust God."

"We all make mistakes, Jack. That's how we learn." She gave him a stern look. "You don't intend to stop telling me you love me, do you?"

"Never," he said. "That would be the biggest mistake of all." He showed her just how much he cared and Gracie responded. They sat in the darkness, sharing the peace that love brings. "You know, after I prayed with Ed, I felt the old burden roll away, but I didn't trust it was gone for good. I kept waiting for someone to tell me I wasn't worthy of love. I didn't think that peace I first felt would stick."

"And it has?" she whispered.

"It was a hard lesson, and I almost let you go

before I realized that if I want the best things in life, I have to trust God's love. That's not risky at all. It heals. You taught me that. Your love has healed both Lizzie and me. You are a very special woman which is why I call you Gracie. You're my Gracie, and I love you more than I could ever say."

"I love you, too, Jack. You are the most lovable man I know." Grace smiled as his arm tightened around her shoulders, pulling her to his side. Here was the answer she'd sought from God for so long. To be loved. To be needed. To have a future purpose.

"When can we get married, Gracie?"

"I can't get married without Jess," she told him. "She has to be my matron of honor, just as I once stood up for her. If it wasn't for Jess..."

"She's coming home tomorrow," Jack reminded her. "The day after?"

"Hmm, maybe a bit after that," she promised.

"You do realize I'm not very patient, that I like to have my own way and that I don't give up easily, don't you?"

"You don't say?" Grace chuckled. She smiled as she peered at the moon. "Isn't it nice that I love that about you, Jack?"

"Gracie," he complained. "When will you marry me?"

She slid her palm to his cheek and held it there, almost overwhelmed by the love that filled her.

God was so good. How could she have ever doubted Him?

"I think we should discuss it with Lizzie tomorrow," she suggested, gazing into those melting tiger eyes she'd adored as a teen. "It will be our first family decision."

"The first of many," Jack agreed happily before kissing her.

Epilogue

On a late summer afternoon in Peace Meadow at Hanging Hearts Ranch, Grace Partridge prepared to marry Jack Prinz.

Neither the announcement in the town hall inviting the community see 'Sunshine's favorite helpful daughter pledge her love to a man quickly becoming the town's favorite son,' nor the presence of the entire town of Sunshine, seated or standing in the meadow, ready to witness their marriage, bothered Grace. She was so happy, she was delighted to share it with everyone.

As flower girl, Lizzie looked adorable in an ankle-length sundress with purple-blue butterflies and pretty white sandals. She led the procession down the grassy aisle with a huge grin below her unruly almost-black pigtails, clinging to a nosegay of dandelions she and her grandfather had picked earlier that day. Jess, dear Jess, glowing with good health, followed behind Lizzie, wearing a lovely purple-blue sheath and carrying white daisies.

Then Grace's precious Calhoun 'boys' escorted her down the aisle. She moved slowly, feeling radiant in her pure white silk ankle sheath, a tiny veil and delicate strappy sandals, carrying Jack's chosen bouquet of violet hydrangeas. Her purple diamond earrings were also a wedding gift from him. Grace had tucked away the tender look on his face when he'd insisted they were not as rare as she was, to savor all through their futures.

After thanking the Calhouns, Grace met her smiling groom eagerly and slid her arm in his, her purple diamond solitaire sparkling in the sunshine for everyone to see.

"You look beautiful, Gracie. As usual," Jack whispered.

"You look like my answered prayer," she whispered back.

Together they turned to face Pastor Ed.

"Dearly beloved..."

She trembled as he began the solemn yet joyful celebration that would unite them. And then Jack's voice, so strong, so certain.

"My darling Gracie, I promise to love you for as long as God gives us. You are my heart, my inspiration, my best friend and the one who makes my days complete."

Jack turned to his best man, Ben, and accepted the ring before solemnly facing Grace. In a clear voice he announced, "With this ring, I thee wed."

He slid the platinum band on her finger while gazing into her eyes.

Then it was Grace's turn.

"My dearest darling Jack. We came the long way around to get here. And yet, it was all in

God's time. I've spent my entire life trying to discern and follow His plan for me, but I could never have dreamed His plan would include you." She stood on tiptoe and kissed his cheek. "I love you. That will never change. I promise to share all the ups and downs of our life as together we seek to follow His leading into our future together." She slid Jack's matching band onto his finger. "With this ring, I thee wed."

"By the power vested in me, I now pronounce you husband and wife. Jack, you may kiss your bride."

Which he did. Thoroughly. Interrupted only by a squeaky voice that mused, "I din't know Pops liked kissin' so much."

The meadow erupted in laughter.

"Ladies and gentlemen, I present to you Mr. and Mrs. Prinz."

Grace grinned at Jack and nodded. Laughing, they grabbed Lizzie's hands and walked down the grassy petal-strewn aisle. Afternoon turned to evening as they shared their jubilant celebration of love at the Double H.

In his toast to the bride, Jack announced that the Prinz family would be settling in at the Herman Schneider home where Grace would pen more children's stories of faith and love while he decided whether a small ranching operation would fit into his photography passion.

Uproarious applause greeted their news.

"But first we're having a honeymoon," Jack

murmured in Grace's ear during their fifth dance together. "We need to leave, darlin'. Now."

Grace kissed Lizzie goodbye, confident she would have fun with the Calhoun children while she and Jack cruised the South Seas.

"That's a stunning suit, Grace. I'm so glad I insisted on that dove gray." Jess's smile mingled with tears and she hugged her best friend in the little log house and then led the way outside. "So now that you're an author, a wife and a grandmother, have you finally figured out where God's leading you?" she teased.

"I know enough for now," Grace told her, locking glances with her new husband. "I can wait for the rest." She hugged her friend close. "I love you, Jess. Thank you for being my friend."

"Right back atcha, kiddo," she said. "Read this later." She tucked a card into Grace's bag, embraced them both one last time and then waved them off in Jack's new car.

As Jack and Grace drove to the airport in Missoula, they chatted about their wedding day and all the things they wanted to remember.

"What's in the card Jess sent?" Jack wanted to know.

Grace opened the envelope. Inside was a beautifully scripted card in Jess's painstaking calligraphy. She read it aloud.

"To every thing there is a season, and a time to every purpose under the heaven… A time to weep, and a time to laugh; a time to mourn, and a time to dance… He hath made every thing beautiful in his time. Ecclesiastes 3:1,4 & 11a."

"That's about as true as it gets, darlin'," Jack declared.

"Yes." Grace put the card back in the envelope to keep it safe. "Whether we have all the answers or not, our future is in God's hands. Right where it belongs. All we have to do is trust that He loves us."

* * * * *

*If you enjoyed this story,
pick up these other stories
from Lois Richer:*

Hoping for a Father
Home to Heal
Christmas in a Snowstorm

*Available now from Love Inspired!
Find more great reads at
www.LoveInspired.com.*

Dear Reader,

Thank you for joining me once more at Hanging Hearts Ranch. I hope you enjoyed Grace and Jack's reunion. After many years of living her faith, Grace worried God was finished using her. Jack had let lies dominate him until he believed he couldn't love or be loved. But fear and love can't coexist. Our couple had to learn that God's perfect love casts out fear. It's a lesson all of us can repeat to bolster our faith in the One who loves us unreservedly.

I'd love to hear from you and I'll do my best to respond quickly. You can reach me via email at loisricher@gmail.com, through my website at www.loisricher.com or on Facebook.

Until we meet again, my wish is for you to share in the boundless love that God our Father gives freely to anyone willing to be His dear child.

Blessings,

Lois Richer